FORGETTING THE EARL

The Arrogant Earls
Book One

Kathleen Ayers

ARE YOU SIGNED UP FOR DRAGONBLADE'S BLOG?

You'll get the latest news and information on exclusive giveaways, exclusive excerpts, coming releases, sales, free books, cover reveals and more.

Check out our complete list of authors, too!

No spam, no junk. That's a promise!

Sign Up Here

www.dragonbladepublishing.com

Dearest Reader;

Thank you for your support of a small press. At Dragonblade Publishing, we strive to bring you the highest quality Historical Romance from some of the best authors in the business. Without your support, there is no 'us', so we sincerely hope you adore these stories and find some new favorite authors along the way.

Happy Reading!

CEO, Dragonblade Publishing

CHAPTER ONE

London, 1836

MISS HONORA DREVENPORT surveyed the crush at Lady Pemberton's ballroom, fluffing out her lavender skirts, then frowning as she examined the more than generous rise of her hips. Gloved hand flapping against one thigh, she silently prayed for the rise of flesh to be smaller. Or at the very least appear much less...*mountainous* than it seemed.

Mama liked to say Honora was full-figured.

Emmagene Stitch, Honora's cousin and dearest friend, suggested she was merely voluptuous, in the way women depicted in Renaissance paintings happened to be.

Emmie meant it as a compliment. Truly she did.

Honora tried to take a deep breath, something she thought might calm her, but she was laced far too tightly, a necessary evil in order to fit in this stupid gown, one her mother had insisted wouldn't complement Honora's figure in the least.

She hated when Mama was right.

Just once, Honora had wanted to appear lovely and swanlike, because tonight, at Lady Pemberton's ball, *he* would be in attendance. Unfortunately, her body wasn't inclined to agree with Honora's vision.

Plump would be the kindest way to describe her figure. Her rounded form combined with a lack of height gave the impression Honora was a tiny teapot, minus the spout, of course. No matter that she starved herself relentlessly in her pursuit to be reed thin or that her mother continuously urged her to try one reduction method after another. Honora's determination and good intentions were often ambushed by a delicious scone. Or a tart.

Blackberry tarts were her favorite.

Generously curved, abundant forms were not currently in fashion and hadn't been in at least a century. Thank goodness today's gowns were far better at hiding a young lady's flaws than the figure-revealing dresses of twenty years ago. Even so, very few gentlemen found a pudgy form such as hers appealing.

She doubted even Culpepper did.

Her lip curled just slightly at the thought of her unwelcome suitor, a gentleman everyone but Honora thought she should wed. Honora very strongly disagreed.

Culpepper's admiration of her had less to do with her person and more to do with the fact Silas Drevenport, Honora's father, owned profitable copper mines and had no son to inherit them. Papa had two daughters: One bright and vivacious, and already wed nearly a year, Marianne. The other...well, the other was Honora.

She thumped her hip again, pleading with the silk to lie smoothly.

"It isn't any use," she muttered from behind a rather large, potted palm that had become her hiding spot for the evening. "I resemble an overgrown hyacinth no matter what I do." Indeed, the roundness of her hips paled in comparison to the rise of her breasts threatening to spill out despite her overly modest neckline. Last year, during her first season, there had been an unfortunate wardrobe incident that had required a cloak and a hurried exit. Most embarrassing. Honora had been laughed at for weeks.

She twisted her fingers. It wasn't the first time she'd been mocked and unlikely to be the last. The world was not kind to chubby, overeducated young ladies.

Pushing aside her thoughts of self-pity, Honora surveyed Lady Pemberton's ballroom with a practiced eye. Scores of perfectly rounded bosoms and tiny waists flitted before her in gorgeous colors. Lovely creamy complexions, not one with a blemish. Honora's face, in comparison, was often marked with imperfections. Nothing on any of the perfect young ladies swirling about resembled a jiggling plate of aspic. If Honora so much as shifted in her seat at dinner, the mounds of her breasts moved as if they possessed a life of their own.

At a small gathering last week in which Honora's sister Marianne had played the piano to much applause, an older gentleman, very unkindly, had drawn a comparison between Honora's bosom and the udders of a cow.

She'd been mortified to have overheard his comments. The wrap she'd brought because the evening was cool had immediately made an appearance.

Honora sighed, batting absently at the palm.

She'd always been chubby. Plump. Liked her desserts far too much. Mama tried to compel her to walk in the park, but Honora often declined. One could not read a book on the Babylonians or Phoenicia while in motion. And Papa, her mother claimed, had overindulged and encouraged Honora's tendencies with books. Trips to the museum and galleries. Attendance at presentations by esteemed scientists, historians, and gentlemen intent on exploring the world.

Gentlemen like the Earl of Southwell.

Honora had found Southwell quite accidentally, though she considered it fate.

She'd asked her father to escort her to a talk being given at the British Museum on India. After all, Papa shared her fascination for exotic locales and interesting historical artifacts. Mama disapproved but allowed her to go. At least she would be walking about.

And there he was. Glistening like a crown jewel in a maharaja's turban.

Honora stared at Southwell in rapt attention the whole time he stood at the podium in the museum's main hall, relating the details of a tiger hunt in India. The rough scratch of his voice flowed over her skin as she drank in the sheer beauty of his face. The tiger was one who'd attacked a score of villagers and had developed a taste for humans. Southwell gestured gracefully with his arms as he sought to make his points, stopping at the right moments to offer an interesting tidbit or personal anecdote. For the entire duration of Southwell's speech, Honora was unable to take her eyes from him.

Papa pronounced himself embarrassed and shocked by her blatant admiration.

Mama finally put her foot down. Honora would never find a husband if she insisted on attending such dry affairs better reserved for educated gentlemen. She could not spend the rest of her life with her nose in a book or looking at dusty mummies and such. Honora argued and pleaded, but Mama could not be swayed. Heartbroken, Honora was forced to pay calls on ladies she didn't even like and attend dull charity teas.

Mama dragged Honora, some weeks later, to what she deemed a suitable event, hosted by Lady Trent and held in that esteemed lady's cavernous ballroom. Donations were being requested for the betterment of orphans, a favorite cause of Lady Trent's, while her guests sipped tepid tea and munched on biscuits. Lady Trent was well known for her charitable endeavors.

Mama didn't have a charitable bone in her body, but she was socially ambitious.

Southwell took the podium, and Honora wasn't the only young lady in attendance to sigh and fan herself.

She had made a point of asking her mother to attend future charity teas as hosted by Lady Trent, because Southwell spoke at nearly all of them. He was a favorite of Lady Trent's and close friends with her son, the Earl of Montieth.

If Mama wondered at Honora's sudden philanthropy, she

didn't mention it; she was far too happy that her troublesome, awkward daughter was finally doing something socially acceptable.

Ah, Southwell. Honora placed a hand over her heart to stop the sudden fluttering.

The Earl of Southwell—or South, as his close friends called him—was everything Honora admired in a gentleman. An adventuresome earl, one who explored the furthest regions of the globe, he had visited some of the most interesting places in the world, often in the company of Lord Carver, head of the Geographic Society. Southwell was commanding. Self-assured. Bold. She had no trouble imagining him holding a rifle aloft as he led his men through a jungle or discovering an ancient tomb buried in the desert. His rugged good looks combined with the sense of danger and excitement hovering about his broad shoulders helped him become the embodiment of her most romantic fantasies.

Honora tugged on her skirts again, ducking as far behind the palm as space allowed. Culpepper was on the move. She could see him circling about, searching for her. The Drevenports approved of Culpepper. He was well connected and moderately wealthy, the sort of gentleman most women of Honora's station would find appealing as a future husband. Neither her mother nor her father could understand her reluctance in accepting his suit.

Southwell entered her field of vision, sauntering across the ballroom like some sleek, sable-haired panther that inhabited one of the jungles he so often visited. His dark formal wear clung to a lean, muscular form kept fit and powerful from his activities. Southwell was so attractive. So unapologetically masculine in comparison to the dandies strutting about Lady Pemberton's ballroom.

Mama insisted that a match with Culpepper would be *splendid*. That was the word she'd used. As if Honora's unwanted suitor was a sunset or a perfect rosebud. Good Lord, Mama had said, did Honora wish to remain a spinster like her cousin

Emmagene? Honora was already—*horrors*—in her second season. Culpepper was more than Honora could hope for given her unfortunate...*silhouette*.

Honora ran her hand over the bulge of her stomach, impossible to see beneath her skirts, but she knew it was there. She was squeezed so tightly in the gown she was terrified she would either faint or split the seams. The palm frond tickled her nose, and she batted it away, distressed to find a bit of her hair beginning to fuzz against her cheek and temple.

Drat. What was the point of using dollops of styling cream to keep her hair sleek? It never seemed to work.

Honora pushed aside the palm frond in irritation. She could no longer see Southwell, and she dearly wished to, but the ballroom was enormously crowded. Anyone of any decent social standing was in attendance. Splashes of color circled the ballroom, bright against the black formal wear of the gentlemen. Lovely hues of rose and powder blue. A confection in cream, dotted with ribbons. Dozens of sparkling diamonds, emeralds, and sapphires graced throats, ears, and wrists. Skirts rustled in time with the snapping of fans. Laughter rose in the air while the musicians, discreetly hidden behind a painted screen, struck up a jaunty tune.

Honora tapped her foot in time to the music. She didn't dance well. Another fault Mama liked to point out.

"Miss Davenport, there you are." A delicate, gloved hand pushed aside the palm frond as Lady Anabeth Wadsworth, daughter of the Marquess of Kendall, renowned beauty, and the most sought-after young lady this season, peered at Honora. Light glittered off the tiny tiara perched on Anabeth's golden curls, nearly blinding Honora.

"Drevenport," Honora corrected her. Anabeth, in their short acquaintance, had never once addressed Honora correctly.

Anabeth's brow wrinkled, making her look like a distraught fairy princess. "Isn't that what I said?"

"No, actually you—"

"Don't you find constantly correcting others to be tiresome?"

Honora pursed her lips to stop her reply. She did find correcting others to be tedious. But she was only trying to be helpful when she pointed out the errors of others. Mispronouncing a word, for instance, or giving incorrect information could have a disastrous effect for both speaker and listener.

"I didn't realize you were looking for me, Lady Anabeth." There was no good reason that Anabeth should be looking for her, though Honora supposed they were friends of a sort. Anabeth and Honora often found themselves attending many of the same charity events hosted by Lady Trent, where Southwell was the speaker.

"Oh, do come out here where I can see you," Anabeth insisted.

Tugging once more on her lavender skirts, Honora reluctantly emerged from behind the palm.

Anabeth took in Honora's carefully styled coiffure, her smile faltering. "Oh, doesn't your hair…look lovely tonight."

"Thank you." Honora patted the side of her tightly constrained tresses, braided and bound to her head with an overabundance of pins. Black as sin and more unruly than a band of orphans, Honora's hair would never behave enough to imitate the elegant style of Anabeth's shimmering curls. Mama had even considered if shaving Honora's head would make the hair grow back in a more normal fashion.

Of course, Mama also wanted to scrub Honora's cheeks and forehead with a brush soaked in lemon water and vinegar to improve her complexion.

"One should be seen at a ball." Anabeth's eyes roamed over Honora's petite, plump form, and she gave a small sniff of her perfect nose. "Your cheeks are a bit…ruddy this evening. Shiny."

"Thank you, Lady Anabeth."

"And the color is very flattering for your complexion." She squinted at Honora's forehead, lips curling in mild distaste as she caught sight of the rather large blemish Honora's maid had tried to hide behind a gathering of curls. "I'm sure you'll be asked to dance if you just come out. You aren't hiding back there, are you?"

"No, of course not," Honora stammered, embarrassed to have been caught doing just that. "I was only taking a moment's respite. The ballroom is quite warm." It wasn't a lie. Moisture was gathering beneath Honora's arms; she could feel the slow slide of it on her skin.

"Is it warm? I hadn't noticed."

Anabeth was the sort of young lady who never worried about unwelcome moisture. Nary a drop would ever *dare* gather above Anabeth's upper lip or trickle between her perfectly formed breasts. It was very unfair.

"Southwell is here." Anabeth tapped her forefinger against her chin.

Honora tried to stop the warmth from flooding her cheeks. "I hadn't noticed." She tried to sound nonchalant, as if she hadn't been staring at him only moments ago. Anabeth knew of Honora's admiration for Southwell as anyone attending one of Lady Trent's tea would. Honora did a poor job of hiding her affection.

"My dear Miss Davenport—"

"Drevenport," Honora quietly corrected.

A tiny wrinkle appeared again between Anabeth's plucked brows. "I'm sure that's what I said. You must have misheard me. At any rate, I'm well acquainted with Southwell, as you know, but you are not. And we are friends, aren't we, Miss Davenport?"

Honora didn't bother to correct her this time. It seemed pointless.

"You're interested in his travels. You *adore* the lectures he is fond of giving while Lady Trent begs us all for donations for one cause or another. I'm sure it isn't just orphans and war widows that compel you to attend such functions."

"The talks he gives are marvelously interesting. I find that—"

Anabeth waved the rest of Honora's explanation away. "Yes,

I'm sure you think discussing tombs and such to be fascinating. I have never been able to garner much enthusiasm." Her fingers landed on Honora's arm. "As much as you esteem him, you've never been properly introduced nor had the opportunity to tell him of your admiration. Wouldn't you like to?" Anabeth's pale-blue eyes twinkled at Honora a bit too brightly. "I know Southwell would be *honored* to know he's inspired you, Miss Davenport. Truly." Anabeth tilted her head, fingers squeezing Honora's arm ever so slightly to make her point.

The crowd parted as Anabeth spoke, enough so that Honora once more caught sight of Southwell.

Southwell threw back his dark head in laughter, the tanned line of his jaw and throat shining in the light of the chandelier, and his features contrasted sharply against the paler faces of the other gentlemen. A glass dangled from one elegant hand, half-forgotten as he spoke.

"Magnificent, isn't he?" Anabeth's tone was wistful. "Though, I do wish he'd find another hobby other than roaming about jungles. It's a dangerous occupation for an earl with no heir." Her gaze landed on Honora once again. "Perhaps he's merely waiting for the right woman."

Anabeth had made no secret of her intent to snare Southwell.

"Come." She took Honora's arm once again. "You mustn't be shy in the least. Southwell adores discussing his travels. He'll be thrilled to find someone who is interested."

Honora dug in her heels, torn between wanting to speak to Southwell and being mortified he'd remember her as the young lady who'd embarrassed herself at a charity tea some months ago. Mama was *still* angry. "I can't, my lady, as much as I'd like to. The ribbon on my slipper has come loose, and I really must retire to fix it."

Anabeth's lips thinned. "I'm disappointed in you, Miss Davenport."

Honora took a deep breath. Most everyone was disappointed in her.

"It is perfectly natural for you to be enamored of Southwell. We all are. There isn't a woman in London who attends those events he speaks at with—" She snapped her gloved fingers. "I can never seem to recall the gentleman's name."

"Lord Carver," Honora whispered. "Of the Geographical Society." Rising excitement over coming face-to-face with Southwell mixed with dread settled in her stomach. She would stammer again. Ask inane questions because she couldn't form a coherent thought.

Her skin would tingle quite deliciously.

"Yes, Lord Carver. As I was saying, most of the young ladies, myself included, enjoy Lord Southwell far more than his lectures. You, Miss Davenport, take pleasure in *both*. There is no shame in admitting it." She tugged on Honora's arm. "Come, you must meet him."

"I couldn't possibly," Honora demurred once again.

Anabeth stopped, regarding her with frustration. "Is your reluctance due to the improper question you asked at Lady Trent's?"

Honora looked down at the floor, studying the tiles. She'd made a complete goose of herself.

"I must admit, I choked on my biscuit when you asked if the crocodiles pulled Egyptians from their boats—"

"Feluccas," Honora whispered as Anabeth pulled her forward, neatly sidestepping a dancing couple.

"—and chewed on them."

"That isn't exactly what I said," Honora protested.

"Quite gruesome of you. Lady Trent looked as if she would faint." Anabeth made a clucking sound with her tongue. "Southwell, however, was intrigued by your morbid nature. I could tell." She paused and gave Honora just the hint of a smile. "You managed to gain his attention. No easy feat. I find myself positively green with envy over the fact."

A tiny thrill coursed through Honora at the thought. "You are mistaken, Lady Anabeth. I'm sure Southwell is quite taken with you."

"True." Anabeth flashed a smile. "But even I have trouble discussing dead bones and other dull topics."

Dead bones? Honora opened her mouth to voice her opinion on Anabeth's choice of words and promptly shut it. Her mother would be proud.

"I *almost* purchased a dull tome on ancient Egypt, trying to stir up some sort of curiosity in Southwell's hobbies. Can you imagine?"

"I cannot." She didn't think Anabeth capable of reading anything other than fashion magazines and the occasional novel. The very thought of her doing so boggled the mind.

"I think such reading to be the providence of elderly scholars. And bluestockings, Miss Davenport, much like yourself. My time is better spent learning the steps of a new dance, I think. At any rate, I doubt he remembers you from Lady Trent's."

Honora didn't see how that was possible. Lady Parker and her niece had swooned at the mention of body parts being strewn about the Nile.

Honora had meant to ask about the Egyptian practice of worshipping crocodiles, something she found intriguing given the obvious danger involved with large, man-eating reptiles. She was fascinated with Sebek, the Egyptian god of fertility who was depicted as a crocodile.

Honora only wanted Southwell's observations. Not even her father wanted to discuss Sebek with her.

The *impropriety* of discussing a fertility god in the company of London's socially moral matrons hadn't dawned on Honora until she'd opened her mouth to speak. And by then Southwell had been smiling at her, striking her dumb with his magnificence. Suddenly at a loss for words, a rare occurrence, Honora could only stammer out a question mildly less appropriate about murderous crocodiles. Blushing furiously, Honora had bravely ignored the startled and horrified gasps of the other ladies sipping tea.

Southwell, oblivious to her mounting embarrassment and the censure directed at Honora, had nodded solemnly, as if carefully considering her question. He'd related several pertinent facts about the Nile's crocodiles, none of which involved them snatching people traveling the Nile on feluccas. He'd stated that hippopotami were much more feared by the ancient Egyptians and because of their vicious attacks, had been hunted nearly to extinction along the Nile.

Southwell had been incredibly polite. Not a bit condescending. She'd basked in his attention.

Nevertheless, it was not Honora's finest moment. Mama, on the carriage ride home, had been livid. Honora was forbidden to read anything else from Papa's well-stocked library. If she were to attend another of Lady Trent's teas, Honora was not permitted to ask questions. She was to put such outlandish interests out of her mind and focus on finding a husband.

Southwell's back was to her as she and Anabeth approached. He was in conversation with another gentleman standing to his left, with sandy hair.

Her stomach roiled. *Oh dear.* Tarrington.

Lord Tarrington and Honora did not care for each other.

She'd made the poor decision to correct him at a party given earlier in the season. Speaking of the United States, Tarrington had incorrectly informed the group surrounding him that Boston was in California.

Honora had gritted her teeth, swearing not to interrupt.

When the topic had changed to South America, Tarrington's idiocy had become even more apparent. Honora had found she could not continue to remain silent. She'd merely *suggested* to Tarrington that Peru was located on the continent of South America and *not* Africa as Tarrington had proclaimed to the circle around him.

The snobbish lord had been livid. He was not appreciative of her timely interruption, nor of her correctly informing everyone that Peru was, in fact, in South America. How could Honora possibly know she'd embarrassed him in front of a young lady he'd been intent on courting?

His displeasure had been swift. For the remainder of that party and any others Honora had the misfortune to attend for several weeks, if Tarrington spotted her, he would follow her about, squealing and snorting like a pig. On one of the rare occasions she'd ventured to the park. Honora had encountered Tarrington. He'd walked by her, murmuring "here, piggy, piggy" until she'd fled. Since then, he had mostly ignored her, and she hoped the worst was over.

Tarrington smoothed down his carefully trimmed mustache as he greeted Anabeth. A look passed between them before he regarded Honora with mild interest.

Honora prayed he had forgotten all about her. She *was* forgettable. Everyone said so.

Anabeth nodded graciously. "Good evening, Lord Tarrington, Lord Southwell." She bobbed prettily. "I've brought a friend to meet you. May I present Miss Davenport."

"Miss Davenport. How nice to see you again." Tarrington seemed polite enough except for the mispronunciation of her name, but possibly he was only repeating Anabeth.

"My lord," she dipped unsteadily.

"Oh," Anabeth laughed softly. "I didn't realize you two were acquainted."

"I believe we met briefly at a garden party hosted by Countess Malvern. Miss Davenport was kind enough to inform me of the location of Peru." Tarrington's tone was bland, his pale gaze flickering over Honora; he was dismissing her.

"Did you think it in Asia again?" Southwell said before turning to Honora. "The tutor his father paid for was a complete waste."

"It was easier to just look over your shoulder during the exams, South," Tarrington bit out. "At any rate, this is Miss Davenport. Brought to us by the lovely Lady Anabeth." He gave Anabeth another pointed glance before nodding to Southwell.

"Drevenport," Honora said quietly. "I am Miss Drevenport."

Tarrington wore a smug look, his eyes on not Honora but Southwell. "Apologies."

Southwell gave her a warm smile before taking her hand, fingers closing lightly over hers. "Miss Drevenport, it is a great pleasure."

The sound of him vibrated down her arm before blossoming into warmth across her chest. He had pronounced her name properly without a bit of gentle correction from her. She might very well swoon.

"My lord." She dipped again as gracefully as she could, praying the seams of this gown would hold. Anabeth and the dreadful Tarrington ceased to exist in that brief moment when Southwell held her hand. Cedar floated into her nostrils, mixed with a hint of leather and tobacco.

"But I think we know each other as well, do we not, Miss Drevenport?" Southwell's lovely brown eyes, flecked with amber, took her in. "But not formally introduced."

Honora nearly puddled at his feet. He released her hand gently, amusement crinkling the corners of his eyes probably because she was staring up at him as if she was addled.

"Lady Trent's charity tea," Anabeth supplied. "I brought Miss Davenport to you because she is a great admirer of those pretty speeches you make."

"You mean she doesn't fall asleep as you do."

Anabeth reddened at his chastisement. "Only once. I was sleepless the night before, and I found the description of the tent you slept in quite tedious."

"It was a yurt," Southwell replied, his gaze still on Honora.

"You've been to Tibet," she said, barely above a whisper.

The side of his mouth tilted, and a dimple appeared in his cheek. "I have. Miss Drevenport obviously doesn't find everything I say to be so tiresome. And I'll warrant she knows where Tibet is, don't you, Miss Drevenport?"

Honora wanted to giggle out loud like a nitwit.

"You"—Southwell leaned just an inch closer to her, so near she could clearly see the brush of hair along his jaw—"are the young lady who asked after crocodiles and hippos. I believe you wanted to know how many unfortunate Egyptians were feasted upon."

"I only asked after crocodiles, my lord. I believe it was you who informed me of the danger of hippopotami, and I don't recall using the word *feasting*."

"I stand corrected." Southwell's eyes sparkled back at her; he was not bothered in the least that she'd done so. "Quite bloodthirsty, aren't you, Miss Drevenport?"

"Miss Davenport absolutely adores the same nonsense you do, my lord," Anabeth interjected. "She might faint with sheer pleasure if you speak of unwrapping a mummy or something equally grotesque."

"Wonderful, we can speak of all sorts of morbid things while we dance." Southwell held out his arm to Honora. "Shall we, Miss Drevenport? Unless, of course, you've promised this dance elsewhere?"

A tiny squeak escaped her lips.

Anabeth smiled sweetly as she nudged Honora. "I'm sure she hasn't."

"My lord, I—" Honora wasn't prepared for dancing, *especially* not with Southwell.

"Are you thirsty, my lady?" Tarrington held out his arm to Anabeth. "Let me escort you to the refreshments. Let's allow Southwell his dance with Miss Davenport."

"Drevenport," Honora whispered as Tarrington and Anabeth wandered into the crowd, thrilled to be relieved of their presence but also terrified she'd been left with the Earl of Southwell. Sweat trickled between her breasts as her underarms became increasingly damp. What if he noticed? What if—

"Miss Drevenport?" He was nodding in the direction of the other couples gathered as the musicians began to play.

Honora looked down at the large, masculine hand, fingers

stretching gracefully in her direction. "Are you certain? I don't dance well," she blurted out.

"Absolutely. I'm an excellent dancer as it happens. I won't allow the slightest stumble. If you step on my toes, I will pretend not to notice, especially if you relate to me why you're so interested in the vicious nature of Nile crocodiles."

"Not any longer. I'm now more concerned with hippos, given the information you imparted, should I ever venture to Egypt, my lord."

"Terrifying to be sure but, as I mentioned, nearly extinct in that region. Why crocodiles, if I may ask, Miss Drevenport?" Southwell whisked her out amid the other dancers, seeming not to notice the interested gazes directed at them. "Is it morbid curiosity as Lady Anabeth implied?"

"Not entirely." Honora lifted her chin at two young ladies who were snapping their fans with envy at the sight of Southwell partnering her. "I was going to ask your opinion about the worship of Sebek."

Southwell didn't bother to hide his surprise. "Bloodthirsty *and* versed in Egyptian gods. You grow more intriguing by the moment, Miss Drevenport."

Honora's heart careened wildly about in her chest as Southwell's hand fell to her waist. No one, not even Culpepper, found Honora intriguing. At the press of his fingertips against the silk of her gown, Honora prayed, as she had never done before, that he couldn't feel the sharp line of her stays nor the bulge of flesh at her hip.

"Has anyone ever told you your eyes are stunning?" Southwell gazed intently down at her. "Like jade."

Another trickle of sweat spilled between her breasts. Were the windows open? The terrace doors? Did Southwell just say he admired her eyes? Was he waiting for her to regurgitate on him her vast knowledge of Egyptian gods?

"I have a sense, Miss Drevenport, that you are having a conversation with yourself, and I would vastly prefer if you conversed with *me*."

"You would?"

"Definitely. Let us discuss Sebek. I rarely find anyone to speak to about such things." A slight frown crossed his lips. "Especially at events such as these."

This was why Honora *could not* and *would not* marry Culpepper. Much like Tarrington, it was unlikely Culpepper even knew the location of the Nile. Or had even heard of Sebek. And even if he had, Mama had expressly forbidden Honora to have even a modestly intelligent conversation with Culpepper, worried Honora might scare him away.

That would be too much to hope for.

"You're doing it again, Miss Drevenport. Having an entire discussion without me," he said with mock ferocity. "I insist you stop doing so immediately."

"My apologies, my lord."

He swept her across the dance floor as if she weighed nothing and wasn't rounded like a tiny bowl one tosses down the green. She bestowed a wide smile on Southwell as they danced by her mother, who fanned herself furiously at the sight of her daughter dancing with one of the most desirable gentlemen in London.

A stone-faced Culpepper stood beside Mama, absently stroking his beard. His annoyance was difficult to miss.

Honora didn't care. She vowed, at that very moment, never to accept Culpepper. In fact, after tonight, she would no longer receive him. Mama would be outraged, but Honora would plead her case to her father. Beg him to allow her to never marry if she didn't wish it.

She tilted her head back to regard her dance partner. Southwell was very tall, much more so when dancing with him versus admiring him from across a room. "I will confess something to you, my lord." How bold she sounded. Self-confident.

"Please do go on. I do hope," he murmured, "this has to do with Sebek." The words, low and silky, wrapped around Honora.

Southwell could induce a woman to do a great many things if

he spoke in such a tone. She stumbled, her heel making contact with his toe.

He barely winced; instead, he twirled her until the skirts of her gown fanned out.

Honora cleared her throat. "I find, my lord, that while I am not averse to crocodiles in principle, my question has more to do with the worship of them by the ancient Egyptians. I find Sebek an odd choice for a—" She paused, feeling very forward to use such a word with Southwell.

"Fertility god?" he supplied helpfully.

"Yes. I've read that some households kept crocodiles as pets, decorating them with jewels and such. It isn't the same at all as having, say...a cat or dog. You never need worry about either of them biting off a limb."

Laughter bubbled from Southwell, a rich, wholly masculine sound like molten chocolate amusement cascading over her shoulders. And Honora did so love chocolate.

"Nor could you take them for a walk or sit them on your lap," she continued, thrilled he found her amusing. No one liked her wit. Mama declared it barely comprehensible.

Another rumble of mirth erupted from him. She caught sight of Tarrington and Anabeth watching them dance from their place by the reception table.

"I must concur, though the thought of someone riding a crocodile down Rotten Row has some appeal, does it not?" Southwell asked.

Honora bit her lip to stifle her own laughter. Unlike the almost sensual appeal of Southwell's amusement, the sound of Honora's own had been compared to the braying of a mule.

"Am I to assume that because Sebek is associated with fertility"—he leaned in—"you found it preferable to be thought of as bloodthirsty? You are a very odd young lady, Miss Drevenport."

"It would have been impolite to ask the question in such esteemed company." Honora decided to leave out the fact she'd been so struck by him she'd found herself unable to think of anything else. "And I suppose most would consider me odd."

"Yes, but I mean it as a compliment. 'Odd' doesn't necessarily mean 'bad.' Just different."

Warmth heated her chest and cheeks.

"By esteemed company, do you mean the elderly matrons who fan themselves and pretend interest while I speak? You're quite right. Can't have them all fainting at once, tripping me as I make my way out, though I'm sure Lady Trent keeps an ample supply of smelling salts and has trained her staff accordingly."

Honora smiled up at him before drawing back, stopping at the sight of her small, gloved hand resting on his shoulder. There was no mistaking the roll of muscle beneath her fingertips. Southwell had not an ounce of padding inside his coat. Unlike Culpepper, who used whatever means necessary to make his form more manly. Once, when he'd paid a call, the padding on one shoulder had slipped down to his elbow.

"I enjoyed your talk on India." She slowly relaxed as they danced, the ease with which they conversed putting aside her fears. Here was a place Honora had sure footing. Most of the things society considered important—marriage, dresses, the weather—Honora cared very little about. Her interests lay in a different direction. Books provided the escape Honora sought from the tedium of a life that fit her as poorly as this dreadful lavender dress. Papa possessed a large collection of travel memoirs, history books, two globes, a wall of maps, and several tomes on archaeology. Her father's library had been Honora's favorite place in all the world until Mama had practically forbidden her to enter.

"I wondered what had sparked your interest."

You did, Honora's heart whispered back to him.

She looked away for a moment to find most of the room staring openly at her clasped in Southwell's arms. Anabeth and Tarrington stood together, though only Anabeth was smiling. Considering she'd set her cap for Southwell, Anabeth looked ridiculously pleased.

A small finger of dread traced down Honora's spine at Anabeth's smile, as if something terrible would happen once she left Southwell's embrace.

"You spoke of a tiger hunt. I found it rather fascinating, though I will admit I am glad to know your aim was off and you missed the tiger."

"Given he was eating his way through a village, Miss Drevenport," Southwell said dryly, "I thought it best he cease snacking on the village's inhabitants. It was unfortunate I failed to bring him down."

"He was only an animal trying to survive," she maintained stubbornly.

"I'm certain you would have felt differently if he tried to eat you. In which case, you might object most strenuously."

"Undoubtedly." Honora's heart was beating wildly within her chest at being held so close to Southwell. More than anything, she wished to freeze this moment in time or at the very least the memory so that she could revisit this dance whenever she wished.

"So is it only Egypt that fascinates you? Or exploration?"

"I love history. Archaeology. Exotic locales."

"I see. It isn't a common hobby among most young ladies."

"Well, I don't paint. Or play the piano. At least not well. I had to do something with my time."

"Both are overrated." A half smile crossed his lips.

"Agreed, my lord. To answer your question, ancient cultures have always engendered my interest. The Egyptians, Greeks, Romans, Babylonians, and the like. I'm also rather fond of the native inhabitants of South America."

"Mayans. Aztecs. Incas." His voice was soft. He pulled her a fraction of an inch closer, still a polite distance but near enough so that her skirts brushed against his legs as they moved.

"Egypt was the first exotic locale I read about," she continued. "That led to mummies. Then the pyramids, scarabs, Sebek, and of course, camels."

"Camels?"

"I'm mainly concerned with how one mounts them."

Something flickered in Southwell's eyes. "Very carefully, Miss Drevenport. I've had the misfortune to ride them across the desert. Horrible creatures. They smell terrible. One sneezed on me." A look of disgust crossed his handsome face. "Ruined my coat."

Honora's lips twitched as she struggled to restrain her laughter, because the sound might cause Southwell to cover his ears and flee.

"Are you warm, Miss Drevenport? I find I am. Some air?" He deftly danced them to the edge of the ballroom, closest to the terrace doors flung open to the cooler air outside. Lady Pemberton's guests lingered in small groups on the terrace. Several couples looked in Honora's direction, surprise that she had been escorted out by Southwell etched clearly on their features.

Honora was more surprised than any of them.

"Have you read Spix, my lord?" she said as he released his hold on her waist, allowing her to take his arm.

The dimple in his cheek deepened. "The German biologist? My word, Miss Drevenport, but you are exceedingly well read." He looked away, back through the terrace doors, as he spoke before returning his attention to her. There was something very akin to regret in his eyes.

"I enjoy books a great deal. Have you read his work?" The unease returned, this time stronger. Not that she anticipated Southwell would do anything remotely improper, they were in full view of the ballroom and the guests on the terrace. But there was now a tense set to his shoulders.

"Of course. I'm only surprised you have." Southwell leaned against the wall, the upper part of his body partially hidden in shadows.

"Only partially. I don't read German, of course, my lord. My father gave me a translated version of Spix's travel through Brazil and the Amazon basin. But only the first volume is in English as

I'm sure you know. I suppose I'll have to learn German should I wish to read the other two. I find his descriptions of the animals and plants of that part of the world very intriguing. Though there are horrible diseases in the Amazon."

"Yes, Spix died of one."

Though she couldn't see his face, Honora could feel the intensity of Southwell's gaze, as if he was studying her.

"There is a recent account by Smyth and Lowe, two of Her Majesty's naval officers. The pair started in Lima, Peru, crossed the Andes, and traveled the length of the Amazon. Fascinating, Miss Drevenport. Have you heard of it?"

"Yes." If her mother continued to forbid the purchase of books she deemed inappropriate, Honora would never get to read Smyth and Lowe's account. She was hoping her father would order a copy.

"Perhaps"—he leaned forward, and Honora caught the mint on his breath—"I shall lend you mine after I've read it." The muted light from the ballroom caught against his features. There was a great deal of confusion stamped on the planes of his face, as if she puzzled him.

"Is something wrong, my lord?"

"No, it's only—" His mouth was mere inches from hers.

Honora became quite light-headed at the thought of touching her lips against his. She immediately shut her eyes, mouth parted, wondering if she'd hit her head and the last hour had been nothing more than a dream. Would Southwell kiss her?

The brush of his lips caught against the skin of her cheek.

She kept her eyes firmly shut, wanting to linger in the moment. Someone was whispering in an excited way on the terrace. She heard her name and Southwell's. Honora reluctantly opened her eyes.

"South, there you are." Tarrington's snide tone came from behind her. "And with Miss Davenport, of all people. You didn't nearly need to go so far." He looked down his patrician nose at Honora. "Lord Carver is here."

"A moment," Southwell said, attention fixed on Honora. Regret colored his eyes.

"But Lord Carver is *here*," Tarrington said pointedly. "This is quite ridiculous. I'm not even sure why we are resorting to such subterfuge."

A gentleman chuckled softly to Honora's left. Two couples were watching her, the ladies laughing behind their hands. Honora dipped her chin sharply, staring at the tips of her slippers peeking out from beneath her skirts. Her stomach pitched, the feeling she was on uneven ground making her legs unsteady. Panic beat against her ribs.

"There is no subterfuge. I am taking the air. I'll join you shortly." Southwell sounded so angry.

"My lord—" Honora started, intending to excuse herself. Something was thickening the air around them, compelling her to flee at the arrival of Tarrington.

"Oh, this is rich," came Tarrington's reply. "You've won, fair and square, South. No need to belabor the point."

"Shut up, Tarrington," Southwell snapped.

"You don't get an extra bit of coin for being out here with her. Good God, aren't you afraid she'll launch herself at you like a bloated warship?"

"Not another word, Tarrington."

Tarrington held up his hands. "Fine. I meant no offense. You've already had your sensibilities offended enough for one evening."

Another snicker. A burst of laughter.

"You should go back inside, Miss Drevenport, and not linger." Southwell turned to her; his words cool. Polite. The easy friendship blooming between them before Tarrington's arrival had dissipated. The tips of his fingers brushed hers. "I enjoyed our discussion and the dance."

Honora blinked against the blinding pain across her heart, hearing the mockery directed at her. This was all some sort of jest at her expense. "I doubt that very much."

"I did, Miss Drevenport. Sincerely." Southwell hesitated before spinning away from her and following Tarrington to the terrace doors. He wandered inside without looking back, likely too embarrassed at having been caught with the utterly disgusting and forgettable Honora Drevenport.

Her palms grew slick, and she had to resist the urge to wipe them against her skirts.

Someone snorted in the darkness, like a pig. She heard her name again. Smothered laughter, as if caught in the palm of someone's gloved hand. Dozens of eyes regarded her through the window to the left of the terrace doors. Lady Anabeth among them, lovely features no longer friendly but distorted by maliciousness.

They're laughing at me. As if I'm an exhibit in a sideshow.

How naive she'd been to think Tarrington had forgotten about the minor slight she'd dealt him. He would never forget. This entire evening, including Southwell's pretended interest, had been nothing more than a heartless prank.

A silent scream echoed inside Honora, shattering every beautiful second of her time with Southwell.

Tarrington's face, alight with glee, was clearly visible through the window. His fingers brushed against his eyes, wiping away the tears cascading down his cheeks from laughing so hard. At her. Southwell stood right next to him.

While Honora watched, Anabeth finally left her position at the window and sauntered over to Tarrington and Southwell. She neatly slid her hand into the crook of Southwell's arm, shooting Honora a satisfied look.

The whispers grew louder on the terrace. Now Honora could make out each word.

"I couldn't believe Southwell took Tarrington's wager to dance with her, the most hideous girl here."

"Good Lord, she looks like an overripe plum."

"Did you see the way she closed her eyes? As if Southwell meant to steal a kiss from her?"

"Southwell's won a hefty purse tonight."

Honora turned toward the garden, clutching the balustrade, hearing the truth of her existence hovering in the air around her. The absolute cruelty of what had been visited upon her nearly brought her to her knees. None of it had been real. Just a joke. A trick played on a pathetically awkward young girl who'd had the misfortune to run afoul of Tarrington.

Southwell.

Tarrington she could understand; he *hated* her. Even Anabeth she had expected would do something awful to her eventually.

He asked me about Sebek.

The kinship Honora had felt with him had been false. A ruse to lure her into dancing. Southwell had made her feel special for the first time in her life, and none of it had been real. It had been nothing more than a wager with Tarrington.

For all her intelligence, Honora was horribly, terribly stupid when it came to Southwell. A tear slid down her cheek, though she tried to stop it.

I will never forget what they've done to me.

Especially Southwell.

Not ever.

"You're out of sorts." Tarrington grinned. "You should be thrilled at the size of the purse you've won. You should also thank me from rescuing you from the little piglet's clutches. Good Lord, she was looking at you as if you were an entire tea tray, which I'm sure she can demolish all on her own. What a sow. The feigned interest in her was a nice touch."

Gideon Lawrence, Earl of Southwell, looked up at Tarrington. How had he not realized, until now, how much he didn't care for his former schoolmate? "What did you do?" He glanced out to the terrace, where a flutter of lavender skirts caught his eye. A group of women next to Miss Drevenport were not so discreetly pointing at her and laughing. "What the bloody hell did you do, Tarrington?"

"Don't tell me you feel bad for the little twit? Come now, I only repaid her for embarrassing me. Stomping about with her deplorable hair and corpulent figure to dictate to *me* on the location of Peru. An obscure country no one gives a fig about." He flicked lint off his sleeve. "I lost the respect of Lady Raynelle Admonton over that little stunt."

"You were destined to lose Lady Raynelle eventually on your own, Tarrington. My dance with Miss Drevenport was a private wager, not a way for you to exact punishment for some minor slight to your pride." Gideon's fists clenched at his thighs; he wished he was already on the ship taking him to Brazil. "Had I known what you had planned, I wouldn't have agreed."

Tarrington shrugged. "Please. You never could resist a wager."

The wagers Gideon had accepted from Tarrington in the past had been outlandish but innocent. Determining the color of a lady's petticoat, for instance. The Widow Helmsworth's had been a dull cream color. Or wagering how long it would take Gideon to bed a new bride saddled with an elderly husband. Never anything cruel.

Lady Anabeth sidled up beside him, her fingers settling on his arm. "Did you not agree to dance with whichever unattractive young lady I brought to your side this evening?" She pouted.

"Yes, but—" It had seemed a harmless bet at the time. Anabeth considered nearly every other woman in London unattractive in comparison to herself. He'd assumed he'd be dancing with an elderly matron, perhaps. Or a lonely spinster grateful for a dance.

"Then why are you angry?" Lady Anabeth declared. "Tarrington suggested Miss Drevenport, and I agreed. She's hideous. I probably would have chosen that self-righteous ball of stuffed satin without his encouragement. Her features are barely discernible amid all that pimply skin. The sheep on the farms of my father's tenants possess better coiffures."

"You used me," Gideon said as self-loathing for his part in Tarrington's scheme filled him.

"What of it? You accepted the wager and won a large sum of money. What you should be concerned about is the damage to your reputation for being seen with that little troll." Tarrington gave a laugh as he smoothed down the ends of his mustache.

"The wager was only to dance with a young lady Anabeth deemed unattractive. A private agreement between gentlemen. I never agreed to making sport of a young lady in front of half of London. Or have you inform everyone at Lady Pemberton's ball."

"Oops." Tarrington pressed a palm against his mouth. "If it makes you feel any better, South, it is doubtful anyone will remember her past this evening's entertainment. She's like a piece of furniture. Or a potted fern. Besides, what are you planning to do? Rush to defend her honor?"

Gideon, much to his shame, stayed silent.

"Miss Davenport waddles about, correcting her betters right and left. She cost poor Tarrington an heiress." Anabeth's fingers trailed along Gideon's sleeve as she nodded toward the terrace. "Not to mention she's annoying. She looks like an overstuffed sausage and is barely worth a moment of your consideration, South. No one, including you, will remember in a week who she is. Or care."

Gideon looked at the beautiful woman hanging on his arm, one he'd once considered marrying. "I understand you are considering the Duke of Denby's proposal," he said casually to Anabeth. She'd been using Denby's interest in her to compel Gideon to offer for her.

"I have." Her fingers tapped lightly on his arm. "Unless you advise me differently." Anabeth's lips formed a pout.

He deliberately plucked her fingers, one by one, from his sleeve. "I think very highly of His Grace. My advice, Anabeth, is you accept his proposal. You'll make a wonderful duchess."

Gideon barely heard Anabeth's gasp of anger as he turned to Tarrington.

"Keep my winnings. I don't want your money or your friendship, Tarrington." Gideon was due to leave for South America in two days. His trunks were already packed.

"South." Tarrington gave him an impatient look. "It was only a prank. I assure you Miss Davenport will survive. She seems incredibly hardy, don't you think? Sturdy, like a large goat."

Gideon didn't answer, so disgusted with Tarrington, Anabeth, and everyone in the ballroom that he could only think of leaving before he suffocated.

Sparing one last thought for Miss Drevenport, Gideon strolled out into the night and his waiting carriage. He couldn't wait to leave England. The creatures inhabiting the Amazon were far less vicious than the ones circling Lady Pemberton's ballroom.

CHAPTER TWO

Almost six years later

Honora Culpepper stood before the mirror in her bedroom, watching in approval as her maid adjusted the hem of her velvet gown. The cut and color were scandalous, to say the least. The gown was a brilliant crimson. It would draw every eye in Lady Pemberton's ballroom.

The neckline was cut low, enough so that one could catch a glimpse of her rounded bosom before the bodice narrowed and fell to her tightly cinched waist. The velvet spilled in folds over her generous curves, giving the impression Honora was sprouting from a blood red rose. Her skin glowed, creamy with just a touch of pink, not a pimple or blemish to be seen.

Very little of the lumpy, awkward young girl she'd once been lingered in the woman she'd become. While she would never be considered willowy, or even slender, Honora had lost the rounded chubbiness she'd once been cursed with, resulting in a seductive voluptuousness that drew the admiration of every male.

It had been a shock to Honora when she'd received her first improper proposal, at her husband's funeral no less. Even more thrilling had been that the gentleman attempting to ask for a discreet liaison hadn't recognized her as poor Miss Drevenport, though they'd been introduced numerous times her first season.

Now gentlemen who would not have even noticed her before praised her wit and intelligence. Her company was sought after. It was a very heady feeling not to be Miss Drevenport.

"Directly after you finish with me," Honora addressed the maid, "feel free to scurry down the stairs and inform *the* Mrs. Culpepper of the indecency of my gown."

Honora's mother-in-law, *the* Mrs. Culpepper, might well have a fit of apoplexy over the crimson gown. A well-deserved collapse. In addition to the other insults Loretta had visited upon Honora, she insisted on being addressed as *the* Mrs. Culpepper. She delighted in pointing out that Honora, married to her son, be referred to as the *other* Mrs. Culpepper, as if Honora was a spare shoe or the least appetizing of two vegetables on a plate.

"Make certain to include how much of my flesh is exposed. I'm tired, you see, of my current lover and am on the hunt for a new one. Perhaps I'll even bring him home." Honora didn't even stumble over the blatant lie.

"Yes, madam."

Honora regarded her reflection, still surprised that the beautiful woman staring back was *her*. It was amazing the changes wrought during her marriage to Culpepper. "What are you waiting for, Gertrude? Scurry along and whisper in *the* Mrs. Culpepper's ear." Honora waved her hands. "Scoot."

The maid bobbed and slid from the room.

Honora's fists clenched against the velvet of the gown. She was no longer of a mind to be browbeaten by the likes of Loretta Culpepper. Besides, all of London now referred to Honora as the *Widow* Culpepper. A beautiful, desirable widow whom no one remembered as pathetic Miss Drevenport. Thankfully. Even Dalward wouldn't recognize her.

Honora pushed aside the loathing at the mere thought of her deceased husband. She hadn't wanted to marry Culpepper, but she had. Indeed, no one had forced her. Not exactly. But the events at Lady Pemberton's ball nearly six years ago had left Honora with few choices and little will to fight her mother's determination she wed Culpepper. The news of Tarrington's wager hadn't failed to reach her mother's ear that night, an embarrassment Mama declared she would never recover from. Marriage to Culpepper had been deemed the only solution by which the Drevenport name could be salvaged, especially once the details of the wager came to light. The most unappealing young lady at Lady Pemberton's ball—deemed to be Honora—must be asked to dance by the Earl of Southwell. The girl in question must be a piglet of such distasteful face and form that Southwell's reputation would be questioned just from being seen in her company. If he failed to dance with this unattractive young lady, he would forfeit a great sum.

Southwell's disgust, Tarrington claimed, had been so great after being in Honora's company that his friend had been forced to flee London for parts unknown because he feared the little, lovesick piglet might throw herself at him in public in an effort to ruin herself.

And Southwell's response? He'd had none. He was gone from England, just as Tarrington claimed.

A fist closed over Honora's heart, squeezing enough so that her reflection winced.

Mama had been beside herself even though the gossip over the wager had abated fairly quickly. After all, no one had really cared overly much for poor, pathetic Miss Drevenport, if they recalled her at all. But in Mama's mind, the stain would linger, eroding the social standing of the Drevenport family. Culpepper came forward, vowing his name would protect Honora from any further humiliation. No one would dare disparage her once she was his wife.

Except him and his mother, of course.

Mama claimed Honora to be most fortunate. After wedding Honora to Culpepper, Mrs. Drevenport had washed her hands of her troublesome younger daughter and focused on the London social whirl. Which was just as well because Honora had no desire to see her mother either in those first few months.

The first time Honora's cousin Emmagene had come to call, she'd been turned away. Culpepper had made a point of informing her that Honora's state was so fragile, so delicate, after what had occurred at Lady Pemberton's, that the least excitement would shatter her sensibilities. He'd declared that no visitors were allowed until his wife regained her health. Honora hadn't been permitted to leave the house.

Just thinking of the four long years she'd spent as Dalward's wife made her hand shake slightly as she smoothed back the sleek coiffure she'd adopted for tonight. Her husband's nightly visits during the first months of their marriage had been full of derision over Honora's affection for Southwell. He'd derided Honora for her undesirability, likening her to a large, fleshy doughball he was forced to copulate with.

Was it any wonder she'd lost her once robust appetite?

Almost two years ago, over dinner, as Honora had picked at the excellent roasted chicken the cook had prepared, Dalward had died. He'd choked on a chicken bone midsentence while mocking Honora for being a barren, worthless wife. One no number of the copper mines her father owned could possibly make up for.

Honora had been suddenly free. Emmie had visited. Plans had been made. All would have been lovely except for the problem of Honora's mother-in-law. Loretta, in a fit of pique and grief, had refused to vacate the premises, stating Culpepper had always meant to leave her this house, not Honora.

Honora had offered Loretta money. Threatened her. Begged Culpepper's sister in Surrey to take Loretta. Nothing had worked. Her mother-in-law continued her campaign of dislike against Honora, going so far as to blame her for asking the cook to make chicken that night and anticipating Dalward would choke on a bone.

Which was so ridiculous Honora had laughed in her mother-in-law's face.

Loretta had declared once more, in case Honora hadn't been listening, that she was barren and worthless.

Exhausted from years of insults, Honora had replied tartly that it was Dalward's fault she was childless. Her current lover would be more than happy to father a child. That was how the lies had started.

Now Loretta assumed Honora was tupping most of London.

She took a breath, though not a deep one, pushing aside the problem of Loretta for another time. When she'd been a new bride, Honora had been so wounded that Culpepper's mother despised her.

Honora glanced at the newspaper on the bed, several weeks old. She had more important things to consider at present. The paper was open to an article announcing the return of the Earl of Southwell to London. He'd been attending to affairs at his country estate for nearly a year after coming back from South America but had finally decided to once more be embraced by the society that adored him. He would be in attendance at Lady Pemberton's ball tonight, an affair held every year without fail.

How fitting.

When Honora thought of Southwell, which was often, she wondered if he even remembered Miss Drevenport, and decided it was unlikely. After all, no one else did. Certainly there had been nothing about her to merit Southwell's regard. She'd merely been a means to win Tarrington's wager.

Ah, Tarrington. It was time for Honora to repay him in kind.

Emmie, who had stormed into the Culpepper home despite Loretta's best efforts, had first put forth the idea of Honora avenging herself on those who were responsible for the long-ago humiliation that had resulted in marriage to Culpepper. Wouldn't it feel good, Emmie had said, taking in Honora's now stunning appearance, to make Tarrington the fool? Shouldn't Southwell feel the pain of having his heart be trampled on? And what about Anabeth?

Emmie's own past experience with love had left her bitter and wishing she'd been able to exact her own vengeance on the man who had broken her heart. But it wasn't too late for Honora.

Emmie couldn't avenge herself, she said, but Honora could.

Fate had already taken care of the former Lady Anabeth, now the Duchess of Denby, far more thoroughly than Honora ever could. Tarrington, the most repulsive gentleman Honora had ever known, would receive his long overdue comeuppance tonight. She'd been planning it for weeks.

But she hesitated over Southwell.

Her fingers brushed the paper, caressing the bold print displaying Southwell's name. Even that slight touch sent a jolt through her.

Honora wanted to lash out at him. Entice him. Discard him. Embrace him. Cast him aside. Her jumbled feelings for Southwell were complicated. She detested him for what he'd done but also longed for him in the same instant. He deserved to feel the same way Honora had. She assumed it would be relatively simple. It was doubtful he'd know her as Miss Drevenport; after all, they'd only spent the length of one dance together. And Honora's looks had changed dramatically. Even her parents had barely recognized her when she'd called upon them after Culpepper's death. And Southwell had been gone from England for five long years. Upon his return, he'd avoided London. Until tonight.

He wouldn't remember Miss Drevenport.

But he *would* remember the Widow Culpepper.

Honora would make sure of it.

CHAPTER THREE

G IDEON LEANED AGAINST his cane, trying without success to ease the ache in the twisted, broken limb that served as his left leg. Cradling the glass of scotch he held, pilfered from Lord Pemberton's study by a nervous servant, Gideon gently flexed his foot, feeling the stretch all the way up his thigh. Along with a multitude of baths so hot Gideon thought his skin would peel off, the stretching helped to ease some of the pain. But not all. That was why he needed the scotch.

He took a sip of the amber liquid and surveyed the ballroom.

The false gaiety surrounding him, full of laughter and careless banter, rang hollow to his ears. Beautiful women strolling by, deliberately arching to display their bosoms, attempted to capture his attention but with little success. Several gentlemen had sought out Gideon, attempting to renew their acquaintance with the Earl of Southwell, but all received only a polite nod followed by as few words as possible. No, he didn't wish to go hunting at their country estate, though it was sure to be splendid. Yes, a house party sounded lovely, but he didn't care to attend. Possibly he would join them for a drink at their club if he found himself with nothing else to do.

London had once seemed bright and exciting to Gideon. There were amusements to be enjoyed. Women to sample. Accolades to receive. Now the city appeared gray and cold. Dull. Boring. Full of people flitting about their frivolous lives with no purpose other than their own pleasure.

A bolt of pain shot up his ruined leg, jerking his body and nearly upending the glass of scotch.

"Jesus," he said under his breath.

Carefully he transferred his weight to his other side, taking advantage of the wall at his back to relieve some of the pressure. The leg stiffened if he stayed standing too long. Or sitting. The only time it didn't bother Gideon overmuch was when he was lying in bed.

Gideon gently bent the knee of his injured leg, feeling the pull of the scars. Another bath would be in order once he returned home from this farce. Steaming water seemed the only remedy for the continuous ache of his muscles.

"Remind me again why I'm here this evening?" Gideon said to the man next to him.

"I compelled you to come." The crisp, precise tone of the Earl of Montieth met his ears. "To enjoy my company." A slight twitch at the corner of his friend's mouth could be either a sign of annoyance or amusement. Gideon had spent years trying to discern the difference.

"You aren't that charming, Montieth." He took another sip of his drink, relieved to find the ache in his leg easing somewhat.

"There are many ladies, several in this ballroom, who would disagree with you."

Gideon took in his imposing friend. Montieth was known for a variety of things, but charm wasn't on the list. "The fact that anyone, let alone a woman, would seek you out for companionship constantly astounds me."

"I've a title and wealth. I could have the personality of an ogre and it wouldn't matter. I'm not sure why I bother smiling at any of them."

"That's a smile?" Gideon took in the twisted lips of his friend. "The creatures swimming in the Amazon are more welcoming than you, Montieth, including the caiman that nearly took off my leg." Gideon winced, repositioning himself again. "Stop making that face. You're frightening the young ladies." He tilted his chin in the direction of three women, all dressed in various shades of pink, like a gossiping bouquet of peonies. "You'll never find a wife if they're terrified of you."

"Nor will you if you continue in your desire to become a hermit," Montieth replied.

This was an old argument, one he'd had with his closest friend many times since his return to England from the Amazon. "I don't need a wife. Or want one, for that matter. I relented and came to London. Isn't that enough?"

"The point of returning to town was to involve yourself in the social whirl. You can't stay cooped up in your house for weeks on end, only seeing me or Carver," Montieth grumbled. "It isn't healthy."

Montieth might appear to others as coldly austere, but inside of his broad chest beat a heart more caring than any mother's. Gideon wouldn't be alive had it not been for Montieth. It had been the stern man before him who'd refused to believe Gideon was dead and had gone to South America to retrieve him. "I can, and I will."

"I didn't sail halfway around the world to retrieve you from the Port of Manaus only to have to waste your life locked in your study, poring over maps."

"I'm not in my study." Gideon lifted his nearly empty glass to the crowd of people before him. "I'm here being bored silly."

"You used to enjoy speaking of your travels, South," Montieth said, frustration coloring his words. "You thrived on entertaining everyone with your adventures, half of which I'm sure you made up."

"Untrue," Gideon countered. "I'm a member of the Geographical Society. I've led expeditions. I've no reason to embellish anything." Once, when he'd been whole, Gideon had led a handful of explorers like himself to map out the far regions of the world. Now he doubted he'd ever leave England again. The knowledge was bitter and pained him almost as much as his leg.

"Half the women in London were enamored of you, South. Didn't one matron swoon when you spoke of the coiled snakes you found inhabiting some ruin?"

"It was a tomb," Gideon corrected him. "And it was giant centipedes. I was so struck by the movements of all those tiny legs I nearly didn't get out of the way in time."

Montieth waved a hand. "Snakes. Centipedes. The point is a woman fainted. Which I'm sure you enjoyed."

"I didn't. The lady in question likely weighed more than you do and wanted me to carry her to the couch to recover."

Montieth's lips twitched again.

"Are you trying to smile, Montieth? It appears as though your mouth doesn't quite know what to do."

"The point I'm making is you used to enjoy the attention of all those women sipping tea and hanging on your every word. Your heroics, embellished or not, charmed a great many of them into your bed as I recall."

"True. I was asked to tea any number of times, and none of those invitations were to enjoy only the scones. But I want to be clear: though there were benefits, I never enjoyed those tedious ladies' luncheons. I always had the impression I was a bit of bread about to be picked apart by a flock of starving pigeons. I only spoke at those functions as a favor to your mother, whom I hold in great esteem, though she does seem enamored of providing for every orphan or soldier's widow in England."

"Lady Trent does love her charities," Montieth said of his mother. "She's busy, at the moment, raising funds for a new wing on a charitable hospital. Can't recall the name. Once it's done, Mother will be onto her next project."

"Your stepfather has the patience of a saint, I think."

"He adores her. But Lord Trent is not without his own eccentricities. My mother has threatened him with bodily harm if he purchases one more horse. The stables are already full. Don't change the subject. You have a duty to your family to consider."

"I like being alone. Solitude suits me. I was an only child, remember?" Gideon tossed back a mouthful of scotch. "And I feel no sense of duty."

The very idea of duty was laughable. Should he feel obligated to his parents? A distant father who seemed to exist only to play cards and entertain his mistress? Or maybe his frivolous mother, who after birthing Gideon, had promptly forgotten his existence and returned to her endless parties in London. Though, he supposed he would need to find something to do now that he could no longer lead an expedition or even join one.

"You should marry," his friend intoned.

"They're all nitwits." Gideon gestured to the young ladies hovering about.

"You're jaded."

"I'm not. The very thought of some mindless ninny floating about my house sets my teeth on edge. What would I do with a wife like that, Montieth? Debate the ribbon on her new bonnet? Discuss how fetching her new riding habit is?" What Gideon didn't say to Montieth was that he doubted any of these gently bred, demure, little twits would welcome the sight of his mangled leg. Even his former mistress, who'd welcomed him with open arms when he'd first returned to England, had been unable to hide her disgust at his disfigurement.

"I'm sure not *all* of them are empty-headed. There's got to be one or two you can converse with."

"The vast majority are," Gideon shot back. "I doubt you could find a woman in this ballroom who even knows where the Amazon is, let alone what continent it's on."

A memory nagged at the edge of his consciousness, of an overweight girl with blemished skin, clothed in lavender. *She'd* been bloody interesting and *not* a nitwit. At the oddest times, the thought of that girl would come to him, along with Tarrington's wager. He couldn't really recall the details of her face any longer except for those exceptional jade eyes. And how he'd unintentionally hurt her.

His fingers curled tighter around the head of his cane.

"You converse with your mistress, South. Not your wife. I barely spoke to Alice."

Montieth hadn't loved his late wife, nor had she cared for him, which was a perfectly acceptable state of affairs among their peers. Unfortunately, Alice had died before providing Montieth with an heir.

"I don't need a wife at all," Gideon assured him. "I've several cousins, any of whom would be more than happy to be the next Earl of Southwell. The difficulty will be in choosing which one is most suitable, since they're all about the same age. That is my sole duty along with having another glass of scotch." He caught the eye of a servant passing by with a tray of goblets. He'd have to coerce the man to bring him a scotch. No easy feat. "But I know you have to remarry, Montieth."

"I do. I have a duty to the earldom. I'm not blessed with a tangle of cousins, and Elizabeth, though I adore her, cannot inherit."

"You'll find someone suitable. What about Miss Benton?" Gideon pointed to a fair-haired young lady who was watching Montieth from beneath her lashes from across the room. "Ancient pedigree. Nice dowry. Loves horses. Your daughter would like her."

"Maybe. Elizabeth is rather picky for a child." Monteith's granite features hardened. "I'll find someone suitable. As should you. I know that things have...*changed* for you, South." His gaze dipped to Gideon's leg. "But you're in danger of becoming dourer than I am. I can't begin to understand—"

"Then don't try," Gideon snapped, cutting off the rest of Montieth's sentence. His friend meant well, but he'd no idea what it had been like to be pulled into all that black water. Unable to see. Or breathe. The terror of feeling the caiman's teeth tearing at your flesh. The heat of your blood swirling around you as it spilled into the water. Gideon still woke up some nights, covered in sweat, a scream on his lips.

"South." Montieth nudged him, eyes full of concern.

"I'm fine. I'm only considering Miss Benton." Gideon flashed him a smile. "*I* don't wish to marry, but we'll find you a lovely bit of fluff to wed, one with limited conversation skills, which shouldn't be too difficult. But right now, let us to retire to the room set aside for cards. It may be the only way I can get another glass of scotch, because I don't think Pemberton's servant is returning." He pushed himself up from the wall, pain lancing up his leg to his lower back.

"How's the leg?" Montieth said quietly.

"Passable." *Excruciating.* "I just need to stretch a bit before we sit down to a hand of cards."

"You're a terrible liar. In fact—" Monteith stopped mid-sentence. A low sound of approval came from him.

"Has that servant returned with my scotch?" Gideon followed Montieth's line of sight, disappointed to see only Lady Pemberton's guests.

A seductive flash of crimson flitted into Gideon's field of vision, weaving in and out of the closely packed crowd. Gentlemen's necks craned. Conversations quieted to low whispers. He watched as the crimson slid along the wall before bursting through the crowd of guests.

Christ.

Hair so black it shone blue in the light of the chandeliers was piled elegantly atop her head. The crimson gown clung to her generous curves in exactly the right way, the skirts waving seductively as she walked. Her bosom, magnificent even from across the ballroom, strained against the tight, fitted bodice of her gown. She strolled about the guests gathered, in a casual manner, as if she was doing no more than walking through the park on a sunny afternoon, not causing a stir at a ball attended by half of London.

The woman turned her gaze in Gideon's direction, delicately curved chin lifted as she boldly assessed him with eyes the color of jade.

Arousal, the sort Gideon hadn't felt in ages, wound itself

around the entire lower half of his body. His cock, which had preferred the company of scotch as of late and not beautiful women, hardened against his thigh.

Miss Drevenport.

The name came to him in a rush, making him almost light-headed. She looked nothing like that young, awkward girl, except for those magnificent eyes. There was no recognition as her gaze slid over Gideon before she turned away.

A gentleman approached her, belly so large the circumference tugged at the buttons of his waistcoat. He waddled with purpose toward her, rudely pushing aside anyone who stood in his way. His florid features belied the fact he was likely already intoxicated. Not unusual, according to rumor.

"There goes Tarrington, prepared to make an idiot out of himself," Montieth said. "He's told everyone Mrs. Culpepper favors him. Wagered, in fact, that she would be his mistress by the end of the evening, and put it in the betting book at White's."

"Mrs. Culpepper?"

"The Widow Culpepper," Montieth answered. "Husband died about two years ago, and she has lately reentered society. I was introduced to her at the theater last month. I'm surprised you haven't heard of her since coming to town. Every gentleman in London is pursuing her."

"I don't get out much. Have you gone after her, Montieth?"

His friend was staring at the vision in crimson.

Montieth shrugged, declining to answer.

Gideon ignored the sudden bloom of jealousy toward his friend before turning back to the sight of Tarrington about to make an idiot of himself over a woman who was bound to refuse him. The years had not been especially kind to Tarrington. He was no longer the handsome, charming lord he'd once been. Gideon found he had little sympathy for Tarrington.

A patient smile crossed Mrs. Culpepper's full, plump lips as she waited for Tarrington to greet her.

Gideon couldn't look away from Tarrington's impending

humiliation. He didn't recognize her; that much was clear.

Mrs. Culpepper extended an arm, allowing Tarrington to take her hand. He immediately pulled her closer.

"How much has Tarrington wagered, out of curiosity?"

"Quite a lot," Montieth said as they watched the scene unfolding in Lady Pemberton's ballroom. "His ego wouldn't allow him to do anything less."

The widow smiled back at Tarrington before wrenching free her hand and deliberately wiping it against her skirts as if to rid herself of his touch.

Tarrington blustered, struck speechless. He composed himself quickly, patent sneer curling his lips even as his face darkened to a near purple with rage. He waved a hand, spitting out words as the curious crowd leaned closer.

"I bet against him," Montieth murmured.

Mrs. Culpepper listened intently, lovely features composed. She nodded at Tarrington. Then she tilted her body in his direction, bosom nearly spilling from her bodice, and whispered in his ear before straightening. The widow laughed right in Tarrington's face. Loudly. Dismissively. The sound full of her derision echoed in the stillness of the ballroom. Even the musicians stopped playing.

Tarrington's eyes bulged, mouth opening and closing like a gutted fish's.

Mrs. Culpepper stared him down, not moving. Daring him to say more.

He didn't, instead turned on his heel, murder in his pale eyes, before marching furiously away while the guests in Lady Pemberton's ballroom snickered and laughed at him behind their gloved hands.

"It appears Tarrington has been dealt a crushing defeat," Montieth mused. "The papers will be full of his humiliation tomorrow."

"I applaud her good taste." Gideon didn't take his eyes from her. She gave a careless shrug as if she hadn't just given a huge set-down to one of society's own and moved in the direction of the refreshment table.

The entire lower half of Gideon's body throbbed in response.

"Introduce me to the Widow Culpepper," he growled to Montieth. "Now."

CHAPTER FOUR

HONORA HAD SEEN Southwell the moment she'd entered the ballroom, her eyes drawn to his lean form like a beacon. Pulse fluttering at his presence, Honora took note of his companion, the Earl of Montieth. She didn't care for Montieth after being introduced to him, finding his chilly personality off-putting. Her sole purpose in making sure she became acquainted with Montieth was so that he would then introduce her to Southwell when the time came.

Her eyes drank in the earl she'd been unable to forget.

The once carefully trimmed sooty hair now fell in a tangled mass to Southwell's broad shoulders. His dark evening wear was still expensively cut. The sculpted planes of his face were just as sharp. But instead of the charming smile he'd once worn, Southwell's lips were pulled tighter, and a weariness had settled itself about him. A cane was clasped in one hand.

He was still as blindingly handsome as before.

A wisp of something raw and primal curled inside her, a pleasurable but unwelcome sensation. Honora didn't want Southwell's presence to have such an effect on her. She put it down to nerves and hastily turned away.

Tarrington must be dealt with first. A few days ago, Honora had nearly decided to let him down gently, feeling some regret over humiliating him in such a public way. But then Emmie had brought her the news Tarrington had once more wagered on

Honora, as if she was some prized broodmare. He'd bet a very large sum that she would agree to be his mistress tonight.

Tarrington was about to be far less wealthy in addition to being mocked.

The huge bulge of his stomach jiggled with every step as he came forward, fingertips smoothing over the full mustache he sported. Thin strands of sandy hair were swept over an increasingly bald pate. His limbs were spindly in comparison to the rest of his rounded form, giving him the appearance of an egg with legs. Though Honora had never liked him years ago, she'd at least found him handsome. But his patrician good looks had since faded. Now his features were clearly stamped with the signs of a gentleman who likes spirits and rich food far too much. Cruelty to others had curled his upper lip into a perpetual sneer. His eyes were filled with greed and avarice. Not to mention his foul breath.

Tarrington's outward appearance now matched his odious personality.

Honora was going to enjoy this, though she shouldn't. She never considered herself the sort of person who would take petty revenge, but in Tarrington's case, she was making an exception. Upon meeting the Widow Culpepper several weeks ago, Tarrington had flirted and made improper comments. Danced with her. Tried to steal a kiss that, quite frankly, had left Honora nearly gagging with revulsion. She'd pretended modesty to put him off. Tarrington assumed she would jump at the chance to reach an understanding with him. During his pursuit, he had never once recognized her. He was so pathetic she'd nearly abandoned her plans to humiliate him at the Pemberton ball. Then Tarrington had wagered on her. Again.

Self-indulged idiot. If she didn't put Tarrington in his place, who would?

"Mrs. Culpepper." Tarrington took her fingers. The very touch of his hand filled her with disgust. Several of Lady Pemberton's guests turned to watch, which was exactly what

Honora wanted them to do. She'd deliberately made a grand entrance.

"Lord Tarrington."

"Mrs. Culpepper, you look divine this evening, if I may say so."

Smug. The very same look Tarrington had had on his face when he'd shamed her at this ball nearly six years ago. Every time he'd snorted and called her a piglet echoed in her ears.

Honora allowed a small, seductive turn of her lips. "And I, you, my lord. I looked for you the moment I arrived."

He puffed up like a rooster about to crow. Honora was half-worried he'd split his waistcoat and she'd be treated to the unwelcome sight of his corseted form, for surely something was containing all that...*fleshiness.*

Tarrington held tightly to her hand, shooting the small groups gathered around them a satisfied smile, certain he'd won not only her but his wager. "Minx." He lowered his voice. "I am as eager as you are to come to an understanding between us. Shall we dance?"

Honora regarded him with wide, innocent eyes before wrenching her hand from his as if he disgusted her. Which he did.

"Mrs. Culpepper, let us not play games. I've made my intentions clear." His eyes left her to glance about the room. Tarrington did so like to be the center of attention, though she was sure this wasn't at all what he'd been planning. "If not a dance, perhaps some cool, night air would suit you."

Honora wiped her hand deliberately against her skirts. "Your meager charms, my lord," she said in a voice just loud enough that those around them could hear, "aren't nearly enough to induce me to take a breath of air with you, let alone anything else. Your ego, I fear, is as inflated as the rest of you."

"How dare you." The pale eyes grew wild.

She leaned forward, whispering close to his cheek, "At least *I* will have won *my* wager, Lord Tarrington. I doubt you can say the same." Honora snorted quietly in his ear. "Here, piggy,

piggy." She straightened, waiting for him to discern Miss Drevenport in the widow he'd pursued for weeks.

Tarrington, the dolt, only gave her a confused look.

How disappointing. It took some of the pleasure out of her revenge to know he still didn't recognize her, but she supposed the memory of Miss Drevenport had faded for Tarrington as it had for everyone else in London. Honora had been barely out when he'd humiliated her. Friendless. Reintroduced to the same people over and over without making the least impression. Years shut away with Culpepper, who'd barely mentioned he had a wife.

Then Honora laughed. Loudly. *Merrily.* Remembering the way Tarrington had laughed so hard at her discomfort that night tears had rolled down his cheeks.

Tarrington's face turned an alarming shade of purple as comprehension flashed in his eyes. "You bitch," he hissed for her ears alone.

The entire ballroom fell silent but only for a moment. Then muted sounds of amusement floated in the air. A lady's giggle came from behind a fan. All eyes were on Tarrington as he stepped back from her, head held high, walking away as fast as his spindly legs could carry him.

She nodded politely to those around before making her way to the refreshment table, hearing the whispers ebb and flow around her. "Oh dear," she said to no one in particular. "I do hope he didn't wager too much."

"That was delightful," Emmie declared at Honora's approach. "I shall never forget the look on his face."

"Nor I," Honora said.

"Feel better?" Emmie looked after Tarrington. "I know I do after what he did to you. And don't you dare feel guilty later. Not for Tarrington. He's a beast. Do you think he finally figured out who you were?"

"Not until just before he walked away. I had to snort like a pig to jog his memory. Honestly, I'm not sure whether I should be offended Miss Drevenport didn't make a lasting impression. And I don't expect to feel any regret over Tarrington."

"You shouldn't. And if you do, I'll be happy to remind you how absolutely devastated you were over the entire affair that culminated in your marriage to Culpepper." Emmie picked up a glass of punch, nose wrinkling as she took a sip. "Disgusting. I do wish the ladies could be served something other than punch or wine."

"You can't be seen drinking brandy and roaming about, Emmie. It isn't done."

Her cousin shrugged. "As if I care. I've already been labeled a spinster. On the shelf. My parents have thankfully given up on me."

Honora had not. Her cousin was known for her scathing remarks, her low tolerance for those she considered tedious— which was nearly everyone save Honora—and the severity of her person. She kept everyone at arm's length, especially gentlemen. Not that there were any who would brave the armor of Emmie's harsh personality. It saddened Honora because the Emmie she knew was loyal. Fiercely protective. Funny, even, when she chose to be.

"I like the flower." Honora nodded to the rose stuck into Emmie's tightly coiled hair.

"My maid insisted, though I told her I didn't see the point. At least I like roses."

The rose was the only concession Emmie had made to soften her appearance. Everything else about her screamed restraint in an effort to stifle what attractiveness she possessed. The gown she wore, a striped blue organza, possessed a high neckline showing not a bit of skin. The sleeves were fitted and closed at the wrist. She wore no other adornment save the rose. Next to Honora, Emmie looked drab and dried up. Purposefully, Honora thought.

"Tarrington is unlikely to forget how I humiliated him this evening, though I still don't regret it," Honora mused. "I'll have to stay out of his way in the future."

"It shouldn't be difficult. He's unlikely to approach you again," Emmie replied. "By the way, have you seen Her Grace, the Duchess of Denby? Her duke was drooling over her as she witnessed your denouncement of Tarrington. His Grace's withered claws were digging into her skin, clutching her to his side. I can't imagine anything worse than sacrificing yourself to such a man on the altar of marriage."

"Plenty of ladies do so, Emmie. Perhaps she loves him."

Emmie burst into laughter. "Honora, stop. I nearly spilled the punch. Love. There's no such thing."

In spite of her marriage to Culpepper, Honora wanted to believe in love. At least in theory. "I always wonder why Anabeth didn't marry Southwell. She was so enamored of him. Everyone was certain they would make an announcement before he left England. I have it on good authority—"

"Whose authority?" Emmie's dark eyes flashed. "Wait, let me guess. My brother's wife. The gossip."

"Virgil has been married for some time, Emmie. Can't you at least try to like her?"

Emmie rolled her eyes in disgust.

"At any rate, according to *Rebecca*"—Honora made a point of emphasizing the girl's name—"Anabeth has been trying to seduce Southwell since he returned last year, but her attempts have proved unsuccessful. His rejection has led Anabeth to suggest Southwell's lack of interest in her is really due to a failing on his part," Honora said delicately. "Which I find hard to believe."

"Because it's Southwell? Your hero?" Emmie snorted.

"He isn't my hero." At least not any longer.

"A fitting end to an unkind rake who should have remained in the Amazon. Don't you dare forget, Honora, what Southwell agreed to. I certainly haven't. He thought you the most hideous young lady that night—"

"Not him but Anabeth," Honora interjected.

Emmie shook her head in frustration. "What does it matter? You cried harder over Southwell than anything Tarrington or

Anabeth did to you." She looked down at her slippers for a moment. "It's the worst sort of betrayal." Her eyes caught Honora's. "Making a woman believe you care when you don't. Using her for your own ends."

Honora couldn't argue with Emmie's logic.

"Worse"—Emmie lifted her chin—"Culpepper used your adoration of Southwell to torment you for the entire length of your marriage. I'm surprised your mother-in-law didn't do the same."

"I don't think she knows. If she did, Loretta would certainly use it against me. She was abroad that year with Culpepper's sister, only returning after we had wed. By then, the gossip was completely gone due to Mother's efforts and my marriage. No one cared what had happened to Miss Drevenport, especially not anyone in London. They'd already moved on to the next scandal."

"Just don't forget the reason you had to marry Culpepper is as much Southwell's fault as Tarrington's. I know, Honora"— Emmie took her hand—"how you imagined Southwell to be...well...*wonderful*. But he isn't. Just remember that when you are introduced."

"I won't forget a thing, Emmie."

"Good, because Southwell is headed this way with Montieth in tow." Emmie raised a brow. "Did he always use a cane?"

"Southwell? No," Honora said absently, smoothing her gown over her hips, a habit from long ago.

"I'm sure he's pretending an injury to garner feminine sympathy. A tactic used by a multitude of rakes to charm women into bed. Don't let him fool you, Honora."

"There isn't a chance of that," she replied. "He's a complete cad." *A beautiful one.*

"What if he remembers you?"

"Tarrington didn't until tonight. Nor did Anabeth recognize me when I saw her at the modiste as I was being fitted for this very gown. She barely glanced in my direction. I made not the least impression on either of them as Miss Drevenport. Southwell is even less observant." A small wince of pressure pressed against her heart. "Possibly if I was an undiscovered species of parrot or the like, he might recall our last meeting." But she wanted Southwell to remember the Widow Culpepper tonight. Become enamored of her. Find her to be the most intriguing and beautiful woman in the room.

"You should make him fall in love with you, then cast him aside." Emmie was watching Southwell approach. "It's the least he deserves."

Her cousin had said such before. "Perhaps I will."

Honora's skin prickled as Southwell neared, sparking along her arms and chest. Why was he still so bloody handsome? Couldn't he have melted into something disgusting as Tarrington had?

A woody scent found its way into her nostrils when he stood before her, patiently waiting for Monteith to make the proper introductions. Southwell possessed the same intoxication for Honora that hot chocolate or scones fresh from the oven once had. A sweetness that burst upon her lips just from looking at him. Her traitorous heart refused to stop flapping about in her chest at having him so close.

"Mrs. Culpepper." Monteith made a small bow. "Miss Stitch."

Monteith's imposing form towered over Honora like some sort of ogre's from a fairy tale. She had to resist the urge to cringe. Even Emmie took a step backward.

"Lord Monteith." Honora gracefully dipped a sharp contrast to Emmie's stiff jerking of her knees. "How delightful to see you in attendance this evening." Her gaze flickered to Southwell with mild interest.

"May I present Lord Southwell, Mrs. Culpepper. Miss Stitch."

The bits of amber in Southwell's eyes sparkled like gold as his gaze took her in, lingering over the exposed skin of her bosom. His perusal, the blatant male admiration, made Honora some-what dizzy, the same feeling she got after a sip of brandy. Leather and tobacco mixed with the light aroma of cedar filled her nostrils as he took her hand. Tiny lines were etched at the corners of his eyes, a testament to years looking out across a sun-drenched horizon far from England's cloudy shores. A dark brush of hair trailed along his jaw, which combined with the hair teasing at his shoulders, gave Southwell a disreputable look.

A quiver shot down her spine. A delicious one.

Outside of Southwell's expensive clothing, there was very little of the earl she remembered. *This* Southwell exuded the same air of capability and command, but there was an edge to him he hadn't worn before. He seemed jaded, and unimpressed with everything around him.

Oddly enough, it only enhanced his appeal.

Emmie tried hard to hide her dislike and failed miserably as she greeted Southwell with a well-clipped, "My lord."

Honora, in contrast, lowered herself just enough that South-well could see directly down her bodice. She straightened gracefully if a bit unsteadily, alarmed at the flush she could feel warming her skin.

"Mrs. Culpepper, a pleasure." Southwell leaned heavily on the cane as his fingers curled around hers. The brush of his lips against her knuckles was more sensual than polite. Or possibly Honora only imagined it to be. However, the press of his forefinger as it trailed along her palm before he released her hand was not fabrication.

Honora reminded herself to breathe.

"I'm delighted to finally make the acquaintance of the famous Lord Southwell." Honora bestowed a brilliant smile on him, instructing her pulse to stop racing about. "Your exploits are well known, my lord." It was practiced flattery, designed to stroke his ego.

The small dimple in his cheek appeared, charming Honora, though she didn't want it to. Southwell seemed far more annoyed than amused by her comment. "More infamous, I'm sure. I fear I'm more cartographer than explorer these days, Mrs. Culpepper."

"You are too modest. All of London buzzes with your adventures. What an interesting hobby for an earl—the exploration, that is, not making maps." Honora was well versed in all things regarding maps and globes, studying such things often and dreaming of faraway places. While mapmaking had been around for centuries, the term *cartography* was relatively new.

His surprise showed. "Are you interested in cartography, Mrs. Culpepper?"

Another ripple pulled at her skin. She could have replied with a mildly flirtatious remark. Or something witty, perhaps. But Honora no longer hid her intelligence, though she didn't flaunt she had the soul of a bluestocking. Most gentlemen's interest was more on the size of her bosom than her intellect. Not Southwell's.

Attraction snapped in the air between them.

"My interest is moderate, my lord. I possess no skills as fine as those required for detailed work such as you do. Were you mapping the Amazon?" She knew perfectly well that was what he'd been doing.

"Yes, it's in—"

"Brazil," she finished for him with a sly smile. "I might not be able to accurately draw a map, my lord. But I can read one. Quite well, as it happens."

Heat sparked sharply in his eyes, all of it directed at her.

A marvelous burst of warmth curled around Honora at having him look at her in such a way. There was no mistaking his interest. "I've always wondered about such faraway places, my lord. The jungles. Wild animals. Tell me, have you ever seen a jaguar?"

"Yes. One with the same color eyes as you possess, madam." His fingers drummed the head of his cane before clasping it tightly again. "More jade, I think. Not emerald." The low purr of his words teased along her skin.

The sound of him, the melody of his voice, hadn't changed.

Even if she were blindfolded, Honora would know the silky tone with its slight rasp of wickedness.

"I like big cats," Honora replied, her reply more seductive than she intended. "Monkeys are also entertaining. Anacondas I find absolutely riveting."

A deep rumble came from Southwell's chest, vibrating down Honora's body to the apex of her thighs.

"You find me amusing, my lord?"

"I find you intriguing," Southwell countered.

"If you'll excuse me," Montieth interrupted in a bored tone. "Lord Maxwell has just arrived, and I need a word with him." He made a short bow to both Honora and Emmie before stomping off.

Emmie gave Honora a pointed look. "I'm going for a glass of punch, though I don't care for it at all. I'll return momentarily." She marched off in the direction of the refreshment table.

"Miss Stitch is—" Southwell hesitated. "—delightful."

It was such an obvious lie Honora nearly giggled. "She doesn't care for events such as these."

"I don't blame her. I don't find them especially diverting myself."

"I don't mind them. I suppose balls and other amusements keep me from becoming lonely. I am a widow, after all." Honora had used this very same bit of speech on Tarrington. He'd lapped it up like a thirsty dog.

Southwell's lips twisted as if he was trying not to laugh. He didn't look at all taken with her practiced words. "I doubt very much that you're lonely, madam."

Honora's fingers tightened against the velvet of her gown. She was lonely. Terribly. Not one gentleman she'd met since Culpepper's death had produced the slightest interest. Because, ironically, the man before her, the one whose heart she wanted— whether to break it or keep it—was still the only man she felt anything for. Why couldn't she hate him? Feel the same revulsion for Southwell as she did Tarrington?

"I don't think you know me well enough to make such an assumption, my lord."

There it was. The challenge thrown down to know her better. Now was the moment Southwell would ask her if she wished to view the gardens. Or possibly he'd be polite and merely ask to call on her. He'd touch her arm and whisper an innuendo. It was what Tarrington had done. What countless other gentlemen had attempted. But she'd encouraged none of them, save Tarrington.

And now Southwell. Because Honora decided seducing him, then tossing him aside might finally break the strange fascination he held for her.

"I stand corrected, madam. My assumption is solely based on the attention you've garnered this evening." His tone held just the slightest hint of mockery, as if he knew her game plainly but would continue to indulge her by playing along. His gaze, heated like the banked embers of a fire, trailed with agonizing slowness down the length of her form.

The ballroom grew several degrees warmer, or possibly the velvet gown was simply too heavy despite the chill in the air. Honora had assumed she could remain immune to Southwell and his bloody magnificence. The heart beating furiously in her chest told her how very wrong she'd been.

Damn it.

"A dance, Mrs. Culpepper?"

Now that was unexpected. Honora looked to the cane at his side, taking note of the tiny brackets of pain around his lovely mouth. The cane was not an affectation. He was injured. Emmie would have told her to begin the humiliation of Southwell by forcing him to dance.

"I'm afraid," she said with a toss of her head, trying to sound flippant, "that all my dances are spoken for this evening, Lord Southwell. Another time, perhaps."

He didn't look the least put out, almost as if he'd known she would refuse him. "I look forward to it." Southwell bowed. "Enjoy your evening, Mrs. Culpepper."

"And you as well, my lord." She kept the polite, slightly seductive smile on her face as he took his leave, even after he'd hobbled away from her in the direction of the room set aside for cards.

"There was no mistaking his interest," Emmie said from beside her, a glass of the hated punch clasped in her hand. "Did he remember you as Miss Drevenport?"

"No." Honora was strangely saddened by that fact. She'd wanted him to. Surely there weren't dozens of widows roaming about spouting off about South America and cartography. But he hadn't. After all, she hadn't been anyone of importance to him then, only the means to win a wager.

She lifted her chin. "He's interested in me, but I didn't care to dance with a lame man."

"Will you try to break his heart? Cast him aside?" A sly smile crossed Emmie's lips.

Honora smoothed the velvet over her hips, a habit she'd never been able to break, though there were no longer mounds of excess flesh to worry her.

"Yes, Emmie, I think I might."

CHAPTER FIVE

HONORA DRUMMED HER fingers atop the desk in her bedroom, staring at one of the hedges in the garden in need of a trim. The gardener, Dobbs, was half-blind, so Honora would need to point out the hedge to him. Dobbs supported a family on his salary and didn't deserve to be fired for an affliction he could do little about.

Her fingers beat across the desk again.

It had been nearly two weeks since Lady Pemberton's ball, and except for catching sight of Southwell across the room while attending a presentation on the Spanish conquest of Mexico, Honora hadn't been graced with the earl's presence. She thought he might be avoiding her. The speech had been attended by only three women, including Honora. Southwell would have been aware she was present. Instead, he hadn't even looked in her direction.

Annoyed at his continued stubbornness—after all, Tarrington had pursued her immediately—Honora had returned home, determined to attend Lady Bratton's ball just so she could dance with a number of gentlemen, none of whom she liked, in order to spur Southwell's interest. Honora had already been in a foul mood when she'd come down for the carriage and when her mother-in-law, perched on the edge of a chair like some giant bat, had seen fit to launch one of her attacks.

Which had prompted Honora to declare she was meeting her

latest lover at the ball. A gentleman she would allow to take any number of liberties with her. It had all been a lie, of course. But it had given her some sense of satisfaction to hear the choking noise Loretta had made as Honora had walked out the door.

Montieth's tall form had caught her eye at several functions over the last two weeks, but Southwell hadn't been with him. So Honora had wandered about and flirted with every randy gentleman who thought a widow of her stature ripe for the picking, hoping word would get back to Southwell and he would seek her out.

He had not.

Honora had been so *sure* of Southwell's interest, but perhaps she'd been mistaken.

With a sigh, Honora turned away from the view of the hedge to leaf through the small stack of invitations on her desk. Perhaps she should have encouraged Southwell more. A fortnight she'd been waiting for him to appear. She'd barely had to try with Tarrington or virtually any other gentleman she'd met since Culpepper had been laid to rest.

Damn Southwell.

The day would best be spent shopping. A new book or two would cheer her up. And while Honora certainly enjoyed torturing Loretta by pretending to have numerous lovers, being hissed at and called a strumpet wasn't the best way to spend her day. Even if she did enjoy Loretta's horror at Honora's supposed lovers. Her mother-in-law, while she didn't leave the house often, kept up her correspondence. Loretta was no doubt painting her as quite the light-skirts.

Making her way to the stairs, Honora directed a footman to have the carriage brought around, before pausing at the voices filtering into the hall from the direction of the drawing room.

A hoarse cackle sent a shiver down Honora's spine. The sound of her mother-in-law's laughter.

A low, male rumble followed, too soft for Honora to make out the words.

Who in God's name could *possibly* induce Honora's mother-in-law to giggle like a schoolgirl? The devil, perhaps? The door had been left ajar, and Honora discreetly peeked through the small opening, mouth popping open at Loretta's guest.

Southwell.

He sat in one of the wingback chairs populating the expensively appointed drawing room, light streaming through the windows, caressing the slashes of his cheekbones and jaw. An ornately carved figurine of a horse sculpted of blue john took up most of the small table next to Southwell. He pointed to the small statue, making a comment Honora couldn't quite hear.

Loretta burst into girlish laughter again.

Honora glared at that horse, detesting everything about the expensive ornament. The blasted thing had fallen on her foot once, breaking her toe. Loretta and Culpepper had been more concerned with the damage done to the horse than the fact Honora couldn't walk properly for nearly two months.

Southwell leaned back against the cushions of the chair, his left leg stretched out, the cane propped beside him.

Not a temporary injury, it seemed. She wondered how he had he been hurt. And when?

A flash of pain tightened his handsome features as Southwell shifted in his seat, foot flexing back and forth as he listened to Loretta blather on. He laughed politely, but the grooves bracketing his mouth remained. A wash of sympathy filled her along with the unwelcome urge to comfort him. She willed it away even as she stepped lightly into the drawing room, making her presence known.

"Honora, *dearest.*" Loretta's brittle greeting filtered out from between her thin lips. "Is that you? I thought you were going out. Don't let us keep you." She waved her hand as if wishing Honora away.

"I didn't realize we had company." Honora slid into the drawing room, her eyes meeting Southwell's. "My errands aren't the least urgent."

Southwell drank her in, challenge lighting his features, daring Honora to make a comment about his sudden appearance in the drawing room.

He had made her wait two weeks. Two bloody weeks. And she doubted it had taken him that long to find out where she lived and get himself invited to tea with Loretta.

Southwell stood with his usual grace, a slight wince the only sign his leg pained him.

"My lord, how nice to see you again." Honora bobbed politely.

"The pleasure is mine." He inclined his head, dark gaze lingering on her mouth.

"I wasn't aware you knew Lord Southwell, Honora," Loretta bit out, clearly displeased by the turn her little tea party had taken.

"We were introduced at Lady Pemberton's ball, by Montieth as it happens," Southwell informed her. "Imagine my surprise to realize there were *two* lovely Mrs. Culpeppers." He shot Loretta a charming smile.

"You are outrageous, my lord." Loretta's wrinkled cheeks pinked.

How disturbing. Honora hadn't been aware Loretta was capable of blushing let alone had blood in her veins.

"I am here on a mission from Lady Trent, who seeks Mrs. Culpepper's"—he tilted his chin in Loretta's direction— "assistance." A soft bit of laughter came from him. "Lord, how confusing this will be. I will never know who answers when I address them."

Another blush washed over Loretta's cheeks as she sipped at her tea, the color stark against her deathly pale features and the black bombazine draping her form. "Do continue, my lord."

"Lady Trent wishes to entice your mother-in-law into a donation for the new wing being built at St. Agnes, a charitable hospital. I also come bearing an invitation for *the* Mrs. Culpepper to attend a tea hosted specifically for St. Agnes."

"I'd be delighted to attend," Loretta said, a biscuit snapping between her teeth.

Of course she would. Loretta rarely left the house, but the lure of being invited by Southwell on behalf of Lady Trent would be impossible to resist.

"I've been asked by Lady Trent to speak to those in attendance about my travels in South America."

"As an inducement for donation, no doubt," Honora said.

Southwell's lips twitched. "No doubt, Mrs. Culpepper. But first, I tried out my speech on your mother-in-law. How have I done so far, madam?"

"Marvelous, my lord." Loretta's teeth flashed, lips pulled back in what one could only assume was a smile.

Honora thought she more closely resembled a rabid dog.

"I hadn't realized Lady Trent held such sway with you, my lord. To have you act as her messenger," Honora said.

"Lady Trent is like a mother to me, and there is no favor she could not request that I would not do for her. She wished *the* Mrs. Culpepper to receive a personal invitation," he said in a solemn tone.

What utter rubbish. But it was as good an excuse as any for him to wheedle his way into seeing Honora. "One wonders why she couldn't be bothered to come herself," Honora said under her breath.

This time, Southwell's lips stretched wide, but he declined to reply.

A hum started along Honora's arms at the sight of that smile.

"Ma'am." Edward, the butler, interrupted their conversation with a soft clearing of his throat from the door.

Loretta turned toward the butler in annoyance. "What is it, Edward?"

"Forgive me for disturbing you, but a note has just arrived from Mrs. Robertson. The messenger informed me the news is quite urgent and he has been told to wait for a reply."

"Bother. What in the world could Winifred need? My daughter in Surrey, my lord. I can't fathom what could be so urgent."

"Of course." Southwell nodded.

Loretta glanced between Honora and Southwell, clearly not happy at the thought of leaving the two of them alone together. "I'll return shortly."

"So," Southwell murmured once the door had shut behind Loretta and as he resettled himself. His forefinger gracefully traced along the arm of the chair, dipping into the crevices carved in the wood as he watched Honora.

She dragged her gaze from the movement. They were just fingers. A hand. Nothing special save they belonged to Southwell. "If I didn't know better, my lord, I would assume you arranged my sister-in-law's note."

"I think you ascribe traits to me I do not possess, madam. Deviousness being one."

"Possibly," Honora replied tartly.

"Then it comes as no surprise to you that I did not come here solely for tea or a donation from *the* Mrs. Culpepper. I consider myself resourceful, madam, but not so much as to have a letter sent from Surrey." The dark sheen of his eyes lingered over Honora.

Honora's skin hummed more deliciously. It was very distracting. As was the insistent pull in Southwell's direction.

"How disappointing." She smoothed her skirts absently, wishing she'd worn something more eye-popping than the plain green dress with its black piping.

"Lady Trent *did* ask my assistance in securing the donation of Mrs. Culpepper." He placed a hand to his chest. "I swear. I only didn't realize there were two of you," he admitted.

"I expected an explorer of your renown to be more thorough in his research."

"Usually, I am. But I found myself impatient. I brought you something, Mrs. Culpepper. Something I think you'll enjoy."

"Other than your company?"

Southwell chuckled. He reached inside his coat, producing a

small, leather tome from his pocket and setting it gently on the table between them. "Given your interest in the Amazon and South America, I thought you might find this entertaining."

A Narrative of a Journey from Lima to Para was stamped in gold along the front of the book. The very same book they'd discussed on that night five years ago.

Her eyes lifted to his, but she saw nothing there. No recognition. Nothing that told Honora that bringing her an accounting of two naval officers in the Amazon basin was anything more than coincidence.

"Thank you, my lord. I would like very much to read this."

"Consider the book a bribe."

"A bribe? Would you not do better to choose flowers or sweets, my lord?" Indeed, neither of those, though expected, would have swayed her in Southwell's direction the way that book did.

And he knew it.

"I would like to take you for a carriage ride tomorrow."

"An intriguing proposition. *If* I were to agree."

Laughter bubbled from him, unpracticed and genuine. The sound was so decadent and lovely. Incredibly male. It did something wonderful to her insides.

"We can speak of anacondas." The elegant fingers once more continued their absent perusal of the carved arm of the chair, dipping and sliding over the wood. He was watching her from beneath his lashes. His mouth was parted slightly, tongue visible between the whiteness of his teeth.

Damn him.

"And jaguars?" Honora said in a breathless way, so unlike her usual speaking voice. He was so much better at this game than her. The air in the drawing room had thickened, nearly suffocating her with the intensity of their attraction to each other.

"And monkeys, if that is your desire."

You. I desire you.

Honora blinked, horrified the words had popped into her

mind. She was supposed to be the seducer. Keep her head while she lured Southwell in and then broke his heart. This wasn't going at all as she'd imagined.

"*Anything* that you wish, madam."

Honora's toes curled inside her shoes. She had to regain control of the situation. Somehow.

When he shifted again in the chair, Honora didn't miss the muffled grunt of pain. "Would you like to take a turn about the gardens, my lord?" she said. Southwell didn't deserve an ounce of sympathy, she reminded herself.

They both stood, but he took longer to come to his feet, clutching the cane and avoiding her gaze as if embarrassed at his infirmity. "A turn about the gardens would be most welcome." He extended his free arm to her.

Honora led him outside, careful to match her steps to his. It was a kindness, one that Honora would extend to anyone suffering, she told herself. She forced herself to think of every year she'd spent with Culpepper. How Tarrington had snorted at her and called her "piggy." The humiliation still lingered inside her, demanding satisfaction.

How I wept at knowing he only pretended to like me.

"Something wrong, Mrs. Culpepper? I have the impression there's a conversation going on inside your head I know nothing about."

Honora's steps faltered. He'd uttered those words to her before. She studied his face for any hint he recalled that night as vividly as she did, but saw nothing. "Not in the least. I was only thinking how to refuse your generous offer of a carriage ride." She glanced at him, unsurprised to find him with that half smile firmly in place. The dimple dipped into his cheek, begging for her touch. "You're very sure of yourself, my lord. What must it be like to be filled with such arrogance, I wonder?"

"You find me arrogant, madam?"

"Terribly," she laughed. "Much like your friend Tarrington."

Southwell's arm stiffened beneath her fingertips. "Tarrington and I went to school together, but we are no longer friends, if we ever were. Nor do I think him a friend of yours, Mrs. Culpepper." A question hovered in his words.

Honora shrugged. Southwell wanted to know if she'd allowed Tarrington liberties with her person, and she had no desire to inform him one way or the other. Let him think what he would. She hadn't known he and Tarrington were no longer friends though. That was curious. Had their friendship ended because of her?

Ridiculous. Southwell hadn't shown Miss Drevenport the least concern that night even while his friends had been mocking her. He was a thoughtless, careless rake, albeit a very charming one. With a bad leg.

Yes, all rakes seduce with a travel memoir penned by two former naval officers.

Honora's skirts brushed against his legs as they moved to a bench set far beneath a weeping willow. The branches of the tree cascaded down, creating a curtain separating her and Southwell from the rest of the garden. "Would you like to sit?"

"Not especially, Mrs. Culpepper." Southwell ducked his head as he wandered beneath the canopy, looking up into the branches.

Honora cautiously followed. They were well hidden from anyone in the house, even if Loretta came out in search of them.

"You prefer to stand? What of your leg—"

The rest of her sentence was cut off by the press of his lips against hers. Warm. Lazy. Like floating down a river on a summer day. Culpepper had been sloppy. Wet. Uncaring whether she participated or not.

Oh, but this kiss.

Nothing Culpepper had ever forced on her felt like this gentle, seductive exploration of her mouth by Southwell. Curving a hand around her neck, he pulled her lips more firmly to his.

A small whimper left Honora. A sound of pleasure she'd never heard herself make. A heady sensation suffused her, spreading across her limbs. The taste of him—tea, mint, and sin (a great deal of it)—settled against her tongue as he coaxed her lips to part. Her heart skipped in an uneven rhythm as his tongue twined around hers and intoxication settled over her shoulders.

Southwell dropped his cane, wrapping his free hand around her waist, and pulled her flush against his chest. A low purr came from him, like a satisfied cat's. Or a jaguar's.

His lips teased against the soft skin of her cheek. "I will assume"—his breath ruffled a loose tendril of her hair—"that is a yes to my offer of a carriage ride, Mrs. Culpepper."

CHAPTER SIX

"WHO ARE THOSE flowers from, Honora? One of your lovers?"

Honora looked up from a riveting account of Lowe traversing a riverbed, snapping shut the book Southwell had given her.

Loretta scowled at her, eyes glittering with hatred as she flicked at the petal of one of the dozen or more roses filling the vase.

"It isn't any of your affair who they are from," Honora answered. "Now, if you will excuse me, I'd like to return to my book." Southwell had sent the flowers, a gorgeous display of crimson roses, just this morning.

"Improper," the older woman hissed.

Culpepper's mother had hated Honora from the moment Loretta had disembarked in London after her lengthy trip abroad, horrified her son had wed without her presence. Never once had she shown Honora a shred of kindness or even an ounce of respect. Though Culpepper had left his mother a sizable fortune from which she could draw a comfortable yearly income, more than enough to purchase a home far grander than this, Loretta refused to leave. Out of spite, Honora surmised.

The skirts of Loretta's black mourning dress rustled as she pulled out one of the roses from the arrangement Southwell had sent Honora, sniffing at the bud. She held the bloom tight in her fist as she wandered to the settee. After fluffing a pillow, Loretta placed it at her back before settling like a giant vulture.

"I demand to know which one of your gentlemen sent these."

"I don't answer to you, Loretta."

The flowers had arrived early this morning with a note, scrawled in Southwell's unmistakable masculine hand, promising he would call for her later in the day. A flutter of excitement filled her chest at the thought of being alone with him for an entire afternoon.

"You're behaving like a harlot." Loretta hissed the word. "Under my roof."

"Don't you mean *my* roof?" Honora sighed in frustration. "You don't own this house, Loretta. I've been kind enough to allow you to stay—"

"Kind?" Loretta carefully pulled each petal off the rose she held.

"You could settle in a lovely home of your own. Maybe move to Surrey to be with Winnie."

"This house has been in my family for—"

"*Fifteen years*, Loretta." The pad of her fingers pressed into the leather of the book she held. "We've debated this since Culpepper's death. This is not an ancestral estate. Not a piece of property handed down through the generations. Culpepper received this house as payment for a gambling debt that was owed to him."

Loretta's face reddened, the lines scouring her cheeks and forehead deepening as she sucked in her outrage at Honora. Her mother-in-law reminded Honora of a toddler who held a breath because his favorite toy has been taken away. One could only hope she would faint and leave Honora in peace.

"Dalward *meant* for this to be my home." Spittle collected on her lips. "Mine."

"Did he? Because he didn't state his desire in his will, which is why we find ourselves in this predicament."

"You probably slept with the solicitor to keep this house. Had my poor son's will altered."

A pounding began in Honora's temples. "You know that isn't

true, Loretta."

"I refuse to allow you to use my home as a den of sin. I fear I'll come home one day to find you seducing one of your lovers on my sofa, as plentiful as they are."

Honora stood with a sigh, clasping the book in one hand. She should have just stayed in her room to read. Honora looked around the drawing room, realizing how little she cared about this house. The thought of just giving it to Loretta chafed at her, but she would eventually do so. Just not today.

"Where are you going, Honora?" Loretta's beady eyes took in Honora's morning dress of pale blue. "Scandalous. You should be in black. I wore nothing else after my Mr. Culpepper died. You're a disgrace."

"Dalward has been dead for two years, Loretta. There is no need for me to wear dark colors. Besides, I've been invited on a carriage ride in the park." She tucked the book under her arm and stared directly at Loretta. "Lord Southwell has invited me."

Her mother-in-law's lips parted, her about to launch into another tirade, but she clamped them shut. "Once he finds out what a tart you are, he won't be sending you roses. I should tell him."

"Do what you must." Honora shrugged, eager to escape to her room and leave the poison seeping out of her mother-in-law. "Enjoy your day, Loretta. I'll have tea brought in."

CHAPTER SEVEN

SOUTHWELL HELPED HONORA into his small, open carriage, a conveyance far more luxurious than Honora had expected. There was no driver or footmen. Honora hadn't considered Southwell would drive them himself today. He wanted privacy, which both surprised and pleased her.

As she settled back against the black leather squabs, delighting in the beauty of the day, Southwell climbed in beside her and took the reins. Her skirts caught on a wicker basket tucked beneath the seat.

"I thought we were merely going for a ride in the park, my lord. Are we having a picnic along the Serpentine, perhaps?" The ribbons of her bonnet fluttered about her neck, and Honora resisted the urge to just throw the stupid little bit of decorated straw from her head. Bonnets made her head quite warm, though they did keep the sun from her cheeks. On a glorious day like today, Honora longed to feel the wind through her hair and was sorely tempted to remove the bonnet. She doubted Southwell would mind.

"We are, Mrs. Culpepper. Having a picnic, that is. But we are not going to the park. I've something else in mind. I thought we could both do with a taste—" He allowed the innuendo to hover between them. "—of the country." The bits of amber in his eyes sparked back at her.

Honora's fingers curled around the edge of her seat. "You're kidnapping me?"

Southwell, especially with the thick dark waves of his hair flowing against his shoulders and the bit of beard he sported, did strike Honora as looking like a pirate. Or perhaps a warrior in an invading army, one bent on making her the spoils of war.

An unexpected bolt of pure desire shot through her. Her grip on the seat tightened.

Her eyes caught at his profile. The slash of cheekbone with the sun glancing off his lightly tanned skin. The aquiline nose. The tiny scar she could see just beneath his ear. There were many gentlemen considered more handsome than Southwell, though he was certainly attractive, but none of those men had his presence.

He caught her studying him and gave her a cheeky wink. "What if I am kidnapping you? Would you like to be my captive, Mrs. Culpepper?"

Yes. "Perhaps," she murmured. It was a rather mild reply from the seductive widow Honora pretended to be but still so close to the truth heat pinked her cheeks.

The busy streets of London faded to be replaced with gently rolling hills spotted with farms and the occasional sheep. She had absolutely no idea where Southwell was taking her. Honora hadn't been out of London in…years. Not since before Culpepper had died. The air around them had grown silent. She imagined she could hear bees buzzing and the butterflies gently beating their wings.

"Tell me about your travels, my lord. I assume we have time."

"A bit. But you must tell me when I begin to bore you."

"When I begin snoring, my lord," came her saucy reply, "you will know I've lost interest."

Southwell gave a soft chuckle before launching into the tale of an Indian prince. A wistful look entered his features as he described the palace he'd visited. The exquisite tiles, the gem-stones studding the walls and decorating the prince's wives. His first look, up close, of an elephant.

Honora closed her eyes, listening to the sound of his voice, envisioning everything he saw, almost experiencing it with him.

He'd traveled to the frontier of the United States, something Honora hadn't known. Southwell spoke of vast plains, all stretching further than the eye could see, populated by giant, shaggy beasts called buffalo. There had been days where his group hadn't seen another living soul, just endless prairie.

Honora tried to imagine such a seemingly infinite, untouched land and couldn't. She wished she could see it for herself. Oddly enough, Southwell didn't mention his last trip, to the Amazon.

"You haven't started snoring yet, Mrs. Culpepper." The dimple in his cheek deepened.

"I'm not the least bored. I could listen to you for hours. And you should call me Honora," she said. "Mrs. Culpepper seems a bit formal considering you have kidnapped me for the purposes of a picnic. And it reminds me of my mother-in-law."

He tilted his chin, mouth only inches from hers. "On one condition will I drop all sense of propriety and use your first name." His gaze dropped to her lips.

"What is your condition?" She thought he might ask for another kiss, something Honora wasn't opposed to giving him.

"You must call me Gideon."

"Gideon," she repeated, liking the feel of his name on her tongue. His thigh had mysteriously found its way next to her hip, the warmth of him searing through the pile of skirts she wore.

"Yes, Gideon." He leaned in, brushing his mouth ever so slightly against hers. "We're here."

Honora inhaled Southwell, catching the hints of cedar and leather before moving back an inch to take in their surroundings. "Where is here, exactly, my lord?" She looked around, seeing nothing but the road they'd traveled on, trees stretching along the edge. There didn't seem to be anyone for miles. "And why would we come all this way for a picnic?"

He stopped the horses. "I wanted to be alone with you,

Honora."

Well, that was rather blunt. "You'll ruin my reputation if anyone finds out."

"No one will. Montieth will claim he was with us the entire day, which we spent with our picnic basket at the park in full view of half of London. Then we had tea with his mother, Lady Trent."

"You're very devious, Gideon." A tendril of anticipation surged through Honora. It was a struggle to remind herself that none of this was real. Could not be real. She was merely making a point with Southwell. Striking a blow for all those poor young ladies with large appetites and hair that puffed like a dandelion gone to seed. Ones who were made mockeries of by beautiful, adventuresome rakes. Her victory against Southwell wasn't just for her, she reminded herself.

Rubbish. Pure and simple. She hadn't been thinking of putting Southwell in his place for at least the last hour. Only of kissing him again.

He stepped carefully down from the carriage, wobbling sharply as his left leg made contact with the ground.

"Gideon?"

"I'm fine," he bit out. Reaching for her, he took her hand. "Look, Honora."

He had stopped the carriage at the top of a hill, one with gorgeous views of green grass sprinkled with a barrage of wildflowers. Beyond the wildflowers, Honora could make out smokestacks and curling gray clouds. They weren't so far from London after all, it seemed.

An oak tree, branches spread wide, was down a small slope, dappled sunlight steaming through the leaves.

"Our picnic spot for today." He nodded toward the tree. "If you will carry the blanket and this"—he pointed to his cane—"I'll tote the basket."

"Are you certain—" She could tell the step from the carriage had hurt him, and they would be going down an incline to the tree.

"I am," he said curtly before taking a deep breath and gripping the basket. "Just hold tightly to my arm." His tone softened. "It will steady me."

He didn't want her pity, or anyone's. Not that she would give it, Honora reminded herself. "A human cane, then? Is that what I'm reduced to?"

A dark rumble came from Southwell. "At present, yes."

They made their way over to the tree, Honora studying the ground to ensure they avoided any rocks or small rodent holes lest Southwell trip. Not that her petite form would be enough to stop him from falling. If he stumbled, perhaps it would be better if he landed atop her, as if she was a well-dressed pillow, to break his fall. A small giggle left her, though she tried to stop it.

"Another conversation I'm not privy to. It's rather offputting." But he didn't sound annoyed in the least. Just curious.

"I was only thinking that if you should happen to trip, I would soften your fall."

"I was thinking the same thing," he said lowly. "Of falling into you." The small half smile appeared as they reached a spot beneath the tree.

Heat warmed her cheeks. She'd been imagining herself more as a sofa cushion than anything else. But didn't she want to sound improper? Seduce Southwell so she could discard him?

Yes, well that was the plan, Honora.

Once they were beneath the branches of the oak, Honora shook out the blanket while Southwell watched, and settled herself atop the checkered wool. The blanket was rather worn, with a corner that looked chewed on. Maybe by some sort of animal. Obviously old. She wondered how many other women he'd picnicked with on this same blanket.

The thought made her fingers twitch.

He carefully lowered himself to the blanket, the frustration at his injury clear, before he stretched out his leg.

Honora wondered, Had he broken it while investigating an

ancient ruin? Had the injury been caused by a poison dart from one of the indigenous people he'd encountered? He'd been chased more than once, according to some of the stories he'd told her on their carriage ride. It wasn't inconceivable that he could have tripped and broken the limb and it had healed badly.

Honora's curiosity was going to get the best of her. "I meant to ask you something, my lord. Before it escapes me."

"Gideon. I'm not much of a lord. I don't do any lordly things."

She fluffed out her skirts. "You are an earl and thus a lord *capable* of lordly things. Whether you wish to avail yourself of such pursuits or not."

"I have always found the life of a titled nobleman somewhat useless." He made a self-deprecating sound of amusement. "I was an only child born of distant parents, and thus the earldom was destined to fall on my shoulders. Yes, I manage the estate, which I'm good at. I don't mind at all visiting tenants or learning the best way to harvest wheat. What I do mind is being idle. Having my only concern be which horse wins a race or what house party I'm to attend. I have no right to complain, of course. I have just always longed for something more."

Honora could understand that. She'd often felt the same way. It was something else she had in common with the Earl of Southwell. "Is that why you started traveling?" She untied the ribbon beneath her chin before carefully setting aside her bonnet. "I did wonder how you became acquainted with the Geographical Society."

His gaze ran slowly over her head to the neat chignon at the base of her neck. "I have always been curious about the world, and I wanted to have a purpose. Being a lord is not a purpose." Southwell's eyes were still on her hair.

Self-consciously, Honora patted the sleek bun, confident none of her wild curls had escaped. But he continued to stare at her so intently Honora reached up again. "Have I something in my hair, my lord?"

"No. I was only thinking how beautiful you are with the sunlight on your face."

Honora exhaled slowly, willing the pleasure she felt at his compliment to fade into the branches of the oak tree. She wasn't used to being complimented, at least not honestly or by someone who mattered.

He shouldn't matter.

The outraged voice inside her head sounded remarkably like Emmie.

"I've made you uncomfortable and didn't mean to. Forgive me?" He sat up and reached into the basket, bringing out a bottle of wine. "Still cool to the touch." Placing it aside, he pulled out two glasses. "Will you bring out the cheese and bread while I pour?"

Honora did as he asked, taking out a small wheel of yellow cheese, a loaf of fresh-baked bread, and two ripe pears. There was also a tart, lightly dusted with sugar, sitting at the bottom of the basket. Honora didn't eat tarts very often these days, mostly because Loretta had banned the cook from making them during the early days of Honora's marriage as sort of punishment for her despised daughter-in-law.

"Would you like to start with the tart? It's blackberry, as it happens." He handed her a glass of wine.

Honora loved blackberry. But it would be better if she didn't. She'd no desire to become round and plump again, a constant worry of hers. Had Loretta known banishing tarts from the menu would benefit her daughter-in-law, she might well have never done so.

"No, thank you," she said, sniffing at the wine. Honora didn't usually partake of alcohol. Champagne sometimes. A brandy after her husband's funeral. Taking a sip, she was instantly taken with the light, crisp taste.

"Tell me about your husband, Honora."

She choked a little on the wine before lifting her eyes to his. "There isn't much to tell, my lord."

"Gideon. I'm curious, though if it pains you to speak of him—"

"It wasn't a love match, if that's what you're asking. He was my mother's choice for me. I had refused him several times in fact, but—" She hesitated, the girl she'd once been wanting to screech at the careless rake she deemed partially to blame for Culpepper. "Suffice it to say ours was a blessedly short marriage." A vision of Culpepper, sneering at Honora before pouncing on her with little warning, flashed before her. The way he'd finished bedding her nearly before he'd started, with little care for Honora's feelings. She knew relations between a man and woman could be pleasurable, but she found it hard to imagine. Her gaze lingered over Southwell, taking in the shape of his mouth.

Maybe not so difficult after all.

"Where did you go, Honora?" Southwell murmured, tipping the wine up to his lips.

Honora drained her glass and didn't answer. She had come to the conclusion that she wanted to seduce Southwell. Or have him seduce her. The exact reason was up for debate.

Southwell lay on his side, propping up his head with one arm, wine glass dangling from his free hand. He was so breathtaking. So…Southwell. What would it feel like to have *him* inside her and not Culpepper?

"You didn't enjoy it," he said blithely. "Not with him."

Or anyone else. Her only lover had been Culpepper. Southwell was likely under a different impression, and she chose not to correct his assumption. "May I have more wine?"

Sitting up, he grabbed the bottle by the neck, filling her glass once more. "A poor situation."

Yes, one I was forced into because of you. Anger at Southwell, for the part he'd played in her misery, resurfaced more loudly than ever. Stubbornly, Honora held on to it. Yes, Tarrington and Anabeth had humiliated her, but Southwell had *wounded* Honora.

"I'm curious about your leg." She didn't want to talk about Culpepper or her awful marriage. The only thing on her mind should be leading Southwell to his own eventual sense of betrayal when she seduced and discarded him. This should be fairly straightforward. Maybe she wouldn't even allow him to bed her. She could merely lead him on and—

Oh, Honora. It's gone far beyond that.

Honora blinked and looked away from the man before her, wishing away the delicate throbbing at the apex of her thighs. No other gentleman's presence had produced even so much as a flutter of her heart. It made her furious.

Gideon sipped from his glass, lashes fanning over his cheeks. "Ask."

"Your leg," Honora replied tartly, thinking of that long-ago night at Lady Pemberton's. "Were you injured in the pursuit of some wild animal?"

"You could say that."

"One who crossed your path through no fault of its own? The poor thing probably deserved to go on its way, with no interference from you." Her voice grew sharp. "But you *tortured it* needlessly."

Just as you did me.

He cocked a brow at her. "You make me sound rather unkind. Intentionally cruel. Perhaps I was only defending myself, if the animal was attacking me. Or maybe—" He paused and continued in a quieter tone, "I merely made a poor decision, as we all do."

Honora narrowed her eyes and took another large swallow of wine. "Doubtful." She decided she liked wine. Why on earth hadn't she been drinking it before now? Doing so might make living with Loretta more tolerable. "You probably needed a trophy of some sort for your study."

"The black caiman who pulled me off the side of the boat I traveled on would have made a fine trophy, but I was worried about surviving rather than making a pair of boots from his hide. When he crossed my path, intent on eating me, I suppose I should have just tossed him a chicken bone and sent him on his way." The length of his jaw hardened, and he was gripping his glass so tightly she thought the stem might break.

She inhaled sharply at the words. Honora had been so focused on the scathing remarks she'd directed toward him she hadn't considered that they might be true. "Gideon—"

"Or I suppose I could have *worshipped* the monster that tried to kill me. Decorated him and kept him as a pet, as the Egyptians did. What was the name of their fertility god?" he snapped at her. "The name escapes me at the moment."

"What?" Honora's own fingers tightened on her glass, terror gnawing at her heart. Southwell had nearly been killed. "You almost died," she whispered.

He matters. A great deal.

"I didn't." He looked away from her. "Apologies, Honora, for bringing up such an unwelcome topic." Anguish clouded his face.

"I asked," she said quietly. "Gideon, I'm sorry. I didn't know or else I wouldn't have been—"

Amber glinted in the depths of his eyes as he regarded her once more. "I don't usually speak of it. I've never even told Montieth what happened, outside the obvious."

Yet he'd told her. Honora's heart constricted painfully in her chest.

"You were right to call me arrogant. I am, or at least I used to be. I had such a belief in my own abilities that I became careless." A brutal note entered his words. "We were mapping one of the smaller tributaries, more a swamp than anything. And not very deep. I was enjoying a brandy, congratulating myself on what an incredible job I'd done and looking forward to reaching civilization, where I could sleep in a bed, preferably not alone." He looked up at her. "Have I shocked you with my honesty, Honora?"

"No." She leaned over and refilled his glass. "Go on." He needed to speak of it; Honora could see it in the way the muscles of his face tightened.

Southwell studied his wine again. "I didn't even have my rifle, which was incredibly stupid. It was late. The moon was only half-full. The water wasn't deep," he said again. "So stupid." His eyes shut firmly, and for a moment, she didn't think he'd continue. "I propped myself up against a crate at the corner. The toe of my left boot was mere inches from the water." When his eyes opened again, he was staring at something Honora couldn't see. "We must have been near a nest, or maybe the caiman was just really hungry. Caiman will often swim past prey at least once, a pass of sorts to determine if the animal is worth eating before attacking. I was too busy patting myself on the back for a job well done to notice the ripples in the water when the caiman passed by the boat. The next time it did so, it came half out of the water, nearly swallowing the whole of my leg, and pulled me under."

Honora's hand shook as she took another mouthful of wine. Caimans as well as crocodiles and alligators took their prey underwater to drown them before feeding. He'd been alone, in that black water, with an enormous beast trying to eat him. "How did you—"

"Survive? I didn't think I would. But I had a knife thankfully, one I wore on my belt. Stabbed it in the eye by sheer dumb luck. I was just thrusting out with the knife hoping to hit him enough times so that he would release me. I was terrified. My lungs were aching to take a breath. I wasn't ready to die."

Honora's heart beat with panic as she imagined that moment. The sheer horror Southwell must have felt. Such a thing changes a person, as she suspected it had altered him.

"When I hit the eye, the beast released me but slowly, dragging its teeth down my leg. I managed to surface, bleeding, knife in hand, and yelled as loud as I could. There were lights bobbing around the boat. McCoy had noticed I was missing."

"McCoy?"

"An American who traveled with us. I was pulled from the water but not before the caiman made another go at me. Scratched me with its front claws. McCoy fired into the water, though I'm not sure he could see much." Southwell looked down into his now empty glass and immediately refilled it. "I shouldn't have told you. It's rather gruesome." He gave her a sharp, angry look. "Don't you dare pity me."

Honora reached out and touched his hand with hers. "I don't, Gideon. Thank you for telling me."

"You should eat." The side of his mouth lifted, though the sadness didn't leave his eyes. "I didn't bring you out here to become completely foxed." After slicing off a bit of pear, he sat up and held the piece to her lips.

"Take a bite." Southwell's fingers brushed against her mouth as he fed her the sliver of fruit. "There's a touch of juice at the corner of your mouth." He leaned over, licking up the drop with his tongue.

Honora's entire body flared softly. "I want to apologize for my earlier comments, which were thoughtless," she stuttered, still feeling the press of his tongue against her skin. Opening her mouth to say more, she instead tasted the blackberry tart as he slid it between her lips.

The same hands that had killed a caiman now fed her a tart. Honora couldn't explain, exactly, why the thought was so erotic, only that it was.

"Why do you smell like a chest of old books?" she whispered.

"I do?"

"Yes. Cedar and leather. A touch of tobacco. I find I like it."

"You are a very odd woman." Southwell brushed his mouth against hers. "Which I find rare and precious."

A rush of warmth spread across her chest. This time, when he lifted a piece of the tart to her mouth, her lips closed around his finger, the sugary flavor of the tart sweet on her tongue.

"You are a sloppy eater, Honora. Look, you've missed a bit once more." His words were low and husky. "Just there." His thumb brushed over the corner of her mouth while his hand cupped her cheek, bringing her head down to his.

When he fell back against the blanket, Honora went with him. Willingly. Her lush curves fitting against the hard length of his body as if they'd come from the same mold. There was no thought of anything but the sensation of his mouth slanting over hers and the taste of the blackberry tart.

His fingers trailed slowly over the curve of one breast, stroking her idly through the fabric of her dress as he kissed her. There was no urgency in the press of his mouth or fingers, just a languid tenderness as if Honora was somehow dear to him.

Her skin pulsed gently where he touched, coming to life beneath his fingers. He slanted his mouth more firmly over hers, nipping her bottom lip until she opened for him. Sucking lightly at her tongue, he licked along the inside of her mouth until she moaned against him.

"Honora," he purred, the vibration rippling over the skin of her neck. One of Southwell's broad hands wandered down across her leg, rifling through her skirts. The warmth of his fingers settled at the hollow of her knee.

"Gideon," she breathed, nearly out of her mind from only a kiss.

"You'll enjoy this. Trust me, Honora."

She could feel the length of him, hard as stone, searing her through her skirts and knew Southwell wanted her. But he made no move to flop her on her back and unbutton his trousers. He was taking great care with her. His fingers continued their path up her silk-covered leg, delicate and light. Honora's breasts had begun to ache as the throbbing between her thighs intensified with every stroke of his fingers.

"Do you want me to stop, Honora?"

God no. She didn't want this afternoon to ever end. "No. I—"

Southwell gently turned her until Honora's back pressed against the blanket, his free arm wrapped around her shoulders. He nipped at the side of her neck, his tongue trailing along her skin until he reached her ear.

Honora trembled as a wave of sensation passed down her body.

The hand beneath her skirts skimmed lightly across the top of her thigh before he pushed her legs apart.

Honora sucked in a breath of air, self-conscious despite how aroused she was. While she was significantly less...fleshy than she'd once been, she was still...*voluptuous*. Culpepper had often compared her thighs to tree trunks, telling her how unappealing they were while wrenching them apart. "Gideon, my legs are—" she stuttered in a horrified voice as his fingers brushed against her underthings.

"Marvelous. Beautiful. Deliciously plump." His mouth caught hers. "I look forward to the day I'm between them."

Honora nearly fainted at the words, though she was mildly disappointed, given the circumstances, that Gideon wouldn't be between her legs *today*. "What are you doing?"

"Exploring." The pressure of his fingers skimming over her underthings sent a shiver through Honora. Culpepper had never touched her in such a way. She gasped when Southwell's forefinger found the slit in the cotton and made contact with her already damp flesh.

She looked up into the branches of the tree, spying two birds who seemed to be watching what was happening beneath them.

"I'm very good at mapping out uncharted areas." His mouth claimed hers again while his fingers, dear lord, his fingers were tangling in the hair of her mound. The butterfly touch across her flesh that followed forced a small whimper to leave Honora's throat. The briefest brush of his thumb against a very sensitive, swollen part of her caused her to jerk. Her legs splayed further apart.

"Gideon—I." Honora had no idea what she was asking for. Her entire body felt tight. Coiled up like a spring. A cry left her as a finger sank inside her, thrusting gently while his thumb toyed with the small nub hidden in her folds. She shamelessly rocked her hips forward, wanting more.

Another finger plunged into her.

"Please."

"I would deny you nothing." Southwell's mouth slanted over hers as he deepened the kiss, their breaths mingling, before his fingers curled inside her, his thumb flicking against her with exquisite care.

A slow roll of the most indescribable bliss rippled down Honora's limbs. Her back arched, hips desperately trying to press further into his hand. She cried out his name so loudly the birds above them fluttered and squawked before flying away. Pure pleasure rained down on her, the sort she'd never imagined or even considered.

Southwell held her in his arms until the last tremor left her, pressing an almost chaste kiss to her lips. His fingers slid from her body. His hand cupped her mound possessively for a moment before trailing back down her leg and straightening her skirts.

"Gideon," she whispered, opening her eyes to gaze into his.

"No one else." The dimple deepened in his cheek.

The unintended truth of his statement punched through the pleasure still ebbing from her body. All other men paled next to the Earl of Southwell. How foolish she'd been to assume she could merely seduce him and toss him aside. That there would be no cost to her. Hurting Gideon would stay with Honora the rest of her life.

And she wasn't sure any longer if she could do it.

He lay down beside her and tucked her into his shoulder, one elegant, capable hand stretching possessively across her stomach. The bits of amber in his eyes sparkled in the sunlight as he and she gazed at each other.

Honora's fingers curled into his coat, her body acknowledging what her mind continued to deny. On that long-ago night, she'd stood before him, unappealing and awkward, and felt...*connected* to him. It was why she'd been so devastated by his part in Tarrington's wager. The connected feeling was back. Stronger. Tighter. As if someone had knotted her to him.

The thought crossed her mind that this entire day might be part of a larger wager on the part of Southwell and Tarrington. After all, she only had his word that they were no longer friends. What if—

"Stop, Honora." He cupped her face, pressing a tender kiss on her lips. "No more conversations with yourself. Or rather, by the look of your face, arguments."

Another shiver went through her at how accurately he'd guessed at her thoughts.

Could she allow herself to trust Southwell? It would mean setting aside the very emotions that had sustained her for so long. Emmie would be furious and declare Honora a complete idiot.

That was the problem with revenge.

Letting go of it was incredibly hard.

CHAPTER EIGHT

G IDEON'S HEART BEAT hard in his chest as he looked into the lovely features of Miss Honora Drevenport, his memory of an overly generous figure, corona of puffy black hair, and blemished skin sliding easily over the beautiful woman he held in his arms.

Did she really think he wouldn't recognize her?

The moment he'd seen her again, strolling seductively across the ballroom in that stunning crimson gown, intent on doing Tarrington harm, Gideon had known her. The jade of her eyes hadn't changed, or her sharp intellect, only the rest of her. Even if he hadn't been convinced, Honora's blithe mention of cartography had pushed aside any remaining doubts.

He pressed another kiss to her lips, savoring the taste of Miss Drevenport. Distrust swam in the green of her eyes. Small bursts of anger, all of which Gideon assumed were directed at him, glittered in the depths. Something mysterious and wonderful crackled between them, but Honora didn't trust it.

The fault was Gideon's.

He liked to imagine he would have mounted some sort of rescue for Miss Drevenport, possibly saved her from Tarrington's petty need for revenge, had he not been on a ship bound for Brazil. It was a lie he liked to tell himself because he was so ashamed of his part in Tarrington's scheme. Truthfully, the careless, young man he'd once been wouldn't have lifted a finger for Miss Drevenport, no matter how inexplicably drawn to her he had been. It had been much easier just to push the incident aside and leave for his next expedition.

Drawn. Such a bland and polite way to explain away the sensation that they knew each other on some deeper, primal level. He'd been able to walk away from the feeling years ago but not now. He adamantly refused. Gideon meant to have her. Every ripe, delicious inch of her.

His cock twitched painfully inside his trousers.

"I should return." Deep pools of fathomless green regarded him. "We don't want to cause a scandal, my lord."

"Yes, it is getting late," he agreed, hating that there was so much left unsaid between them. He suspected Honora's reluctance in not admitting who she was meant Gideon was destined to receive the same treatment as Tarrington one day. It wouldn't be a difficult task for Honora. Gideon was already half in love with her.

Gingerly he stood, testing out the weight on his injured leg, watching the sun bathe her face in gold as she repacked the basket.

She smiled up at him before standing, holding out the basket. Gideon grabbed the wicker handle while Honora bundled up the blanket and picked up his cane.

"Will you be needing this?" She held the cane aloft. "Or will I do?"

"You will do perfectly fine," he said quietly, the words filled with meaning. Guilt pulsed through him at what a young, thoughtless lord had been party to. He'd abandoned her to Tarrington that night.

Tell me, Honora. Scream at me. Hit me.

Her lips parted as if she would say something, but instead Honora only took his arm, squeezing her to him. "Will you tell me more of your travels? I promise not to snore. I've questions, you see."

Gideon pressed a kiss to her temple. There was a light, floral scent that clung to Honora. Not lavender. Something more exotic. "I have no doubt. Yours is an inquisitive mind." Another wave of desire for her struck him.

She gave him an impish smile. "I wanted to ask about the fish with teeth."

"Piranha? The ones who can rip the flesh from a man's bones in minutes?"

Honora nodded, leaning her head against his shoulder as they walked.

"Good lord, you're a morbid little thing, aren't you? I'll tell you, but first, do you mean the piranha that live in the Amazon or the ones floating about London?"

Her laughter, throaty and slightly seductive, filled the air. "Both, I suppose."

CHAPTER NINE

S OUTHWELL CALLED THREE days after their picnic, surprising her with his arrival because he hadn't sent a note ahead. And because she'd thought he would call sooner given the intimacy of their afternoon picnic. But Southwell had sent her a gift despite his absence. Not flowers but another book, a rather obscure one. Written in Greek. It had arrived just after breakfast yesterday.

Honora didn't read Greek, which Southwell had probably guessed. He'd meant to pique her curiosity with a tome written in the language, which he had. Everything about Southwell intrigued her. Which she suspected he also knew.

"My lord." Honora's heart leaped at the sight of him, decked out in a coat the color of tilled earth, the same rich hue as his eyes. She said a silent prayer of thanks that Loretta was confined to her room with a headache.

Southwell came forward, fingers curling over the head of his cane as he bowed.

Heat flared in her cheeks as she remembered how those elegant fingers had curled and fluttered inside her. She'd thought of little else.

"Mrs. Culpepper." There was a seductive edge as he addressed her, made more pointed by the way his gaze lowered to her mouth. "I've come to take you to the museum. A new trove of Egyptian antiquities is on display. We will have only today to view it before the entire exhibit is open to the public. I'm certain," he said, barely above a whisper, "you'll be enamored."

She already was. Of him. Honora had spent several mostly sleepless nights thinking of Southwell and what she should do. When she'd concocted her little scheme, which truthfully now seemed ridiculous in the extreme, Honora hadn't expected to find herself so desperate for him.

"I adore the museum as I'm sure you've guessed." The British Museum was one of her favorite places to while away an afternoon, something she'd done frequently before wedding Culpepper, but during her marriage, she'd been forbidden from going.

"You look like a woman who appreciates a good mummy."

When Southwell teased, smiling at her as he was doing now, with the delectable divot in his cheek, Honora's very bones melted. "I do, my lord. The dustier, the better. As I'm sure you've guessed. I'll get my things. It will only take a moment. Would you like tea while you wait?"

"No." He caught her with one arm as she passed him. Southwell's nose dipped into her neck, his breath tickling against her skin. Pressing an openmouthed kiss below her ear, he murmured, "I've missed you, Honora."

"You should have called." Her knees buckled just slightly at his touch.

"I sent a bloody book. In Greek."

She'd been right about the book. He had meant her to send for him after receiving it. "Yes, but I don't read Greek. I'll only be a moment," she said, turning her chin until her lips brushed along his jaw.

Southwell's grip on her tightened. A low rumble came from him before his hand trailed down her spine to her waist. "Don't tarry. I can't leap up the stairs as I used to."

Honora's cheeks burned all the way to her room. She'd managed to calm herself before coming back down the stairs, where Southwell waited.

Once they were settled in the carriage, this time with a driver, he rapped on the roof. "Take us through the park first."

Honora raised a brow. "I thought viewing the exhibit was a matter of some urgency, my lord. Won't this route take much longer?"

He slid across the aisle, tossing his cane on the seat he'd just vacated. "Christ, I hope so." He trailed his fingers along her jaw, stopping to skim her lips before bending his mouth to hers.

A soft sound came from Honora's throat as she wrapped her arms firmly about his shoulders. His tongue rasped against hers, mouth urgent and hot; he kissed her as if he hadn't seen her in three years, not a mere three days.

Southwell pulled her into his lap.

The play of his mouth against hers became deeper. Lush. He feasted on her lips as the carriage rocked and swayed through the park. A small groan left him as she wiggled, intentionally, against the pulsing heat beneath her. She slid her hands inside his coat to caress the hard muscles of his stomach.

"Don't do that," he growled, taking his mouth from hers. "Else I'll take you here, in this carriage. You'll miss all the lovely mummies. And bloody pottery. Or a sarcophagus."

"Well, that changes everything." She tried to push herself off his lap. "The mere mention of a sarcophagus immediately cools my ardor."

"No. Stay." His arms tightened their grip as he pressed a kiss to her temple. "Just try not to bounce around so much. It's sheer torture."

Honora sighed, placing her head on his shoulder. She threaded her fingers through the thick sable hair brushing his shoulders. "Your hair is unfashionably long, my lord. It suits you."

Another low rumble came from his chest.

When they finally arrived and exited the carriage, Southwell escorted her inside. He stopped before an unimportant-looking side door and knocked. The door opened to reveal an older gentleman, who bowed low to Southwell and nodded politely to Honora before gesturing for them to follow him down a deserted hall.

This part of the museum was empty. Quiet. Their footsteps echoed on the marble floors until they reached a set of double doors. Taking a key from his pocket, the gentleman, whose name was Mr. Filbert, opened the door.

"I'm sure I don't have to tell you, my lord, but please no touching," Filbert said before handing Southwell the key.

"Of course, Filbert. I'll keep my hands to myself." Southwell winked at her. "That doesn't include you, madam."

Filbert looked scandalized but nodded politely and left them to explore the cavernous area, filled with all sorts of antiquities, themselves.

Honora sneezed at the dust still lingering in the air. "When did you say this will be open to the public?" She waved her hand. "I don't believe the cleaning crew has been through, Gideon."

"Tomorrow. But everything is set. The artifacts are marked with tiny cards." He pointed out one such note before a small case of glass beads. "We can read them as we go along."

Southwell seemed not to need the cards. He paused at each display, whispering to Honora everything he knew about whatever relic was there, which was quite a lot.

"Have you been involved in this exhibit? You're very informed."

He shrugged. "Come look at this mummy."

The Earl of Southwell was the only person Honora could imagine who could make embalming sound wicked. Or a set of hieroglyphics. Each time he murmured a fact to her, he took the opportunity to touch the tip of his tongue to her neck. Or nip the lobe of her ear. Or press a kiss to the pulse beating in her throat.

Honora was aroused before they even arrived at the sarcophagus.

In her opinion, Southwell was a gifted speaker. A mapmaker. An explorer of distant places and cultures. But after an impassioned recitation on the pharaohs of the Eighteenth Dynasty, Honora realized he was also a scholar. He would never be solely content merely haunting London's gentlemen's clubs to play cards or discuss horses and mistresses.

Not once in the nearly three hours they spent discussing, coughing at the dust, and observing did Southwell ever treat Honora with a hint of condescension. He delighted in her curiosity. Encouraged her to follow her interests. Debated historical facts with her, never once deriding her opinion.

Honora's heart stretched forcefully in his direction, reaching for Southwell and no other.

"Thank you for this, Gideon."

He kissed the tip of her nose. "You're welcome. There is a café nearby if you'd care to stop before I return you home."

She nodded and took his arm. "That would be lovely."

They left the exhibit and went back to the main hall, which was now filling with all manner of people. She was giggling over a story Southwell was relating to her about a large cricket he had found inside his trousers while sleeping in the desert.

Abruptly Southwell halted and pulled her behind him. He gripped the cane tightly in one hand.

"South," came a snide voice, sounding even more horrid in the cavernous space of the museum. "Fancy seeing you here. I've called on you several times, but you never seem to be at home."

"Tarrington," Southwell bit out.

Tarrington's pale eyes slid to Honora. "You've been occupied, it seems, by the lovely Mrs. Culpepper. She's very entertaining. I know from experience."

Honora glared at him. *Vicious, lying swine.*

"Somehow I doubt that," Southwell replied casually, as if Tarrington hadn't just boldly insinuated Honora had slept with him. The very thought made her stomach turn. She refused to allow him to upset her. She gently touched Southwell's back, the warmth of him steadying her.

"Now, if you'll excuse us." Southwell tried to lead Honora away, but Tarrington stepped before them again.

"I'd be careful if I were you, old friend. Mrs. Culpepper is full of secrets, aren't you? Though I'm sure you have some of your own, don't you, South? Anabeth told me the caiman did more than leave you with a scar or two." He nodded at Southwell's thigh.

Southwell gave Tarrington a bland look. "Good day, Tarrington." He jerked, pulling Honora in the direction of his carriage, walking far more swiftly than a partially lame man should be able.

The thought of Anabeth...and Southwell. An awful, hollow feeling pressed into Honora's stomach. She stumbled, trying to wrench her arm from his. "Gideon, wait."

"You'll cause a scene, Honora. That's what Tarrington wants," he said as they approached the carriage. He helped her in before climbing onto the leather seat across from her, the cane clutched in one hand. Southwell's features were tight. Grim. Pain bracketed his mouth, and Honora knew the headlong rush out of the museum had hurt his leg.

"I've seen the duchess only once since my return."

"I didn't ask. Nor is it any of my affair." Honora laced her fingers together, twisting the digits about in agitation.

Southwell's gaze fell to her lap before returning to her face. "Yes, but you should listen all the same. I am in the habit of soaking in a hot bath every night because of my injury."

"Sounds lovely."

"One night"—his voice raised—"I was soaking and having a scotch when I was interrupted by Anabeth, who wore nothing but her chemise."

"How seductive." If his intent was to reassure Honora, he was failing miserably.

"I'm not sure which one of my idiot servants let her in, probably my butler. I think women intimidate him somewhat, and—"

"Oh, good Lord, Gideon. Get on with it. I don't need to relive every moment of her seduction."

He glared back at her. "I left my bath and told her to vacate the premises. Immediately. I may have thrown a bedsheet over her. And yes, I was quite naked. I was in a bath."

"I assumed you were naked." Just the mere thought of Southwell without clothes sent a rush of longing through her in spite of her anger. "Nor is it *any* of my affair."

Brave words. Complete lies. She half expected him to ask about Tarrington's horrible accusation, but he didn't, probably realizing there was no way Honora would ever stoop so low.

His fingers drummed impatiently against his thigh. "It *is* your affair. It pains me that you can sit there and pretend it is not."

"There is no need to explain yourself, my lord," she replied coolly. "We are not—"

"Do not say another word, Honora." His anger echoed loudly in the confines of the carriage. "You have no idea what we are. Or what we could be. And if you are wondering if I am fully functioning, despite Her Grace's denouncement of my manhood alluded to by Tarrington, the answer is yes. I am. I just didn't care to bed Anabeth."

"Again, it is none of my affair." She refused to look at him and instead turned her gaze to the window, willing away the vision of him and Anabeth together.

A hiss of frustration left him. "Shall we discuss Sebek, Honora?" he said in a dangerous tone. "Why don't we?" He waved a hand at her. "Never mind. Do your worst."

Her head jerked from the window. If he knew her as Miss Drevenport, why didn't he say just say something? "I think you've given me enough of Egypt and their gods for one day, my lord. I feel a headache coming on. Please take me home."

"As you wish." Gideon closed his eyes, effectively ending any further conversation.

Honora returned to looking out the window until the house she shared with Loretta came into view. Once the carriage halted, the moments ticked by as she waited for him to say something, at least bid her good afternoon, but Gideon remained silent and tight-lipped, anger coming off him in waves.

Finally, Honora swung the door open herself as a footman rushed down the steps to help her descend.

Gideon did not offer to escort her inside.

CHAPTER TEN

S OUTHWELL DIDN'T CALL the remainder of the week, and after the poor ending to their day at the museum, Honora didn't expect him to. She assumed his interest in her had waned completely, but another book had arrived just today. The dusty tome with torn pages looked as if it had been sitting on the back shelf of someone's library for the last century. There were detailed drawings of various plants. Trees. One whole section was devoted to beetles. Notes in Gideon's masculine hand were scribbled in the borders.

It was the second volume of Spix's work about the Amazon, written in German.

Honora had held the book to her chest before carefully placing it on the shelf in her bedroom, wishing for an end to the confusion and muddled feelings heaped around her heart.

Now, as she made her way to the drawing room, where Emmie awaited to accompany her to Lady Trent's ball tonight, Honora realized several things at once.

First, her jealousy of Anabeth was unwarranted. Justified, perhaps, but wholly unnecessary. Any encounter Gideon may have had with the Duchess of Denby had been well before his courting of Honora.

Second, Honora had to admit to herself that Southwell *was* courting her. Gently. Carefully. There wasn't any denying it. If he'd been bent only on seduction, he could have had her beneath the oak tree. Honora wouldn't have stopped him.

Lastly, tonight Emmie expected Honora to discard Southwell in front of everyone in attendance at Lady Trent's ball. A few weeks ago, Honora would have assumed the same thing.

"Don't you look divine." Emmie held a small snifter of brandy aloft. "I helped myself. I hope you don't mind. I may have shocked Edward."

Honora didn't mind in the least. "My butler is used to being shocked." She gave her cousin a weak smile.

Well?" Emmie said.

"Well, what?" Honora glanced at her cousin, garbed far too severely for a ball.

"I'm once again corseted and clothed in satin with the sole purpose of watching you wreak havoc on a deserving gentleman. What you did to Tarrington was nothing short of exquisite. I can't wait to see you do the same to Southwell." She picked up her wrap. "Shall we?"

Honora ignored her cousin's enthusiasm, declining to move toward the door. "How do you move your arms?" She took in Emmie's dark-blue silk. "It looks as if you had the modiste sew you into the top half of your gown."

"I've not the assets"—she nodded at Honora's bosom—"you do, cousin." Smoothing down her skirts, Emmie said, "I expected to find you much more excited about tonight. Triumphant, as a matter of fact. Southwell is enamored of you, according to my gossiping sister-in-law. I suppose you'll discard him when he asks you to dance, dropping hints about his manhood." A choked laugh escaped her. "It is turning out better than I could imagine."

"I suppose." Honora glanced down at her hands. None of what had happened with Southwell was meant to be real, yet—it was. That was the other belated conclusion she'd come to.

"So how will you do it? It's my understanding that your friend Anabeth—"

"She isn't my friend as you well know."

"I meant it facetiously, Honora. Her Grace, the Duchess of

Denby, claims Southwell's *affliction*"—a smile crossed her lips at the word—"is due to a terrible injury he sustained in the Amazon."

"What an incredibly improper and questionable assumption for you to make." The last thing Honora meant to do was discuss Gideon with Emmie.

A soft rustle met Honora's ears, and she turned toward the drawing room door, relieved to find it empty. "We should go, Emmie."

"Is it true?" Emmie leaned in. "Is he unable? I heard he's scarred—" Emmie waved her hand down across her thighs. "—there. Possibly his leg wasn't the only thing ruined." She leaned in, eyes alight with curiosity. "Imagine breaking his heart and ensuring he's an object of pity. I couldn't have planned it better myself."

Honora ignored her speculation and headed through the doorway. "Keep your voice down. I'm not sure Loretta is abed yet. Nor do I wish the servants to overhear." Honora had felt the hard press of Southwell against her thigh when they'd kissed. Seen the way his trousers had strained after...well, after their picnic. No, Southwell wasn't impaired. Not in the least.

Emmie scowled back at her. "What difference could it possibly make?"

"Madam." Edward appeared from the depths of the house with her wrap. He bowed. "Miss Stitch."

"Not one more word, Emmie, until we're in the carriage." Honora strode out the door Edward held open for her, her cousin at her heels. Once they'd settled in the carriage, Honora took a deep breath and looked Emmie directly in the eye.

"I'm not going to break his heart tonight, Emmie," Honora said quietly.

"I understand. Why bother? The gossip the duchess has already started by claiming he is only half a man will do far worse. You won't have to do a thing but ignore him. The rumor mill will do the rest. As it did with you. Brilliant."

Honora stayed silent as the carriage began to move.

"How will you do it? Dismiss him after a dance?"

"He doesn't dance, at least, not any longer. I think you're missing the point I'm trying to make."

Emmie tapped her mouth with her forefinger. "It would be perfect to watch him limp around you. Maybe have him bring you punch and fling it in his face? Then decry him for not being a man? That will be lovely."

Honora sent her cousin a sharp look. Emmie's dislike of Southwell had evolved into hatred, the sort that Tarrington practiced. Her dislike was a direct result of having consoled Honora over what had happened, and Emmie's own past.

"You're a good friend, Emmie. The best." Honora took Emmie's hand, squeezing her fingers. "I hope you know how much I love you."

"I do." Emmie's smile froze on her face, her excitement fading. "You aren't going to do it. Oh, Honora." Her cousin sat back against the squabs, disbelief on her features. "You've fallen for him again, haven't you? He's *using* you. Why can't you see that? For all you know, you are part of another wager with Tarrington."

Hadn't Honora considered that very thing herself?

"Don't come to me weeping when he humiliates you again," Emmie said as Lady Trent's house came into view. "Which he will. You're making a huge mistake."

Honora stepped out of the carriage. "It is mine to make."

CHAPTER ELEVEN

HONORA WANDERED THROUGH the crowd at Lady Trent's, searching out the tall, lean gentleman leaning on a cane, but there was no Southwell to be found. She knew, by the admiring glances cast in her direction, that the striped silk gown, one shade deeper than the jade of her eyes, had been an inspired choice. The neckline was somewhat indecent, showing a good portion of her bosom. Once, before she'd felt beautiful, showing off her skin had been a novelty, as had the admiring looks her bosom garnered. Now she only cared that one man appreciated her appearance.

Gideon would love her in this gown. At least, she hoped he would. Emmie's warnings still rang in Honora's ears as she made her way around the perimeter of the room, alone. Her cousin had stomped off the minute they'd arrived, probably to terrorize a debutante or servant that crossed her path.

"Still so handsome, though I do wish he'd cut his hair." A feminine sigh caught Honora's ear. "Pity about the cane. He once danced so beautifully. I had the pleasure some years ago."

The words stopped Honora in her tracks. She paused, looking at the two women, whose backs were to her. Difficult to discern their identities without seeing their faces. The clipped, snobbish tone was vaguely familiar.

"I'm sure he doesn't use it for everything." A fan flapped sharply, along with a giggle. "The Duchess of Denby's comments in that regard are nothing more than her trying to salvage her pride. She's been tossing herself in Southwell's direction for as long as I can remember but to no avail. Poor dear. Now look at her. She's the most miserable duchess I've ever seen. Denby keeps her on a short leash, allowing her very little freedom until she produces an heir. I'm not even sure how she snuck out to see Southwell."

"Carefully, to be sure."

Honora turned slightly, catching sight of Anabeth, Duchess of Denby, the girl who'd pretended to be her friend but whose only intention had been to help Tarrington embarrass and humiliate Honora.

Anabeth's elderly husband stood beside her, looking down his thin nose at all who greeted him. When Anabeth tried to move away to speak to a young lady waving in her direction, Denby's arm shot out, his hand wrapping around her wrist as if she was an errant child. Or a whipped dog. Honora recognized the misery in her eyes. She'd seen it in her own when Culpepper had been alive.

"Lord Anders," said the woman in front of Honora, "is all but throwing his daughter at Southwell. But our adventuresome earl doesn't seem inclined to catch her. I don't blame him. She's as dull as dishwater."

Honora caught a glimpse of the speaker's profile. Lady Wainwright. She'd been introduced to Honora months ago while walking in the park. She didn't recognize Lady Wainwright's friend.

"I understand all Southwell's attention is taken by Mrs. Culpepper. The two of them—" Lady Wainwright's fan stopped midflutter as she caught sight of Honora behind them.

"Don't let *me* interrupt." Honora gave them both a knowing look. "But I do feel the need to correct you on one point," she murmured as she sailed past. "He definitely doesn't require a cane...for *that*."

Lady Wainwright gasped at Honora's audacity, but Honora

paid her no mind. By the end of the evening, her little comment to Lady Wainwright would be all over London. If anyone was to disparage the Earl of Southwell, it would be Honora and no one else.

Finally, Honora saw him, standing just inside the terrace doors. Her pulse ticked up a bit, fluttering softly in her neck.

Southwell gestured with one hand as he spoke to a rumpled-looking giant of a man beside him, Southwell's movements graceful and sure, no matter the cane at his side. He was so handsome Honora's breath caught at the sight.

He'd seen her out of the corner of his eye, watching him. The half smile appeared as Southwell's arm lowered, his free hand stretching out in invitation to her.

Honora didn't hesitate. If he hurt her this time, she would have only herself to blame. The responsibility was hers alone. Ignoring the snide looks and curious stares, Honora made her way to him, giving all of London the confirmation that she and Gideon were lovers. Not that they were. Not yet.

When his hand closed over hers, peace filled her.

"There you are, Mrs. Culpepper." He pulled her closer, hiding their clasped hands in the folds of her skirts. "I thought I'd have to hobble through this entire overblown affair to find you. And I mean that kindly. I adore Lady Trent but not events such as these."

"But exploration and discovery are your strong suits, my lord. You would have been able to find me with little difficulty, I think."

"I disagree," he rasped against her skin, his voice warm like molten chocolate. "It took me far too long to find you."

She heard the catch in his voice. Southwell didn't mean tonight.

"Do not say it, Honora. You have no idea what we are. Or what we could be."

But she did. She knew exactly what they were to each other.

CHAPTER TWELVE

"**M**RS. CULPEPPER, MAY I introduce you to my cousin, the Earl of Huntly."

Honora didn't offer her hand to the Earl of Huntly because it would require releasing Gideon's. But it was just as well because Lord Huntly didn't seem inclined to take it.

Montieth had previously been the tallest gentleman of Honora's acquaintance, but Huntly put Montieth to shame. Where Montieth was tall and lean, with a loose-limbed elegance, Huntly appeared a craggy, unscalable mountain, one in which gloomy clouds persistently hovered over its peaks. There was a stain on his waistcoat—wine, she thought. His hair, the color of a tarnished gold coin, fell in an unruly mass about his ears and cheeks, catching on his poorly shaved jaw. The *only* thing remotely lovely about Lord Huntly was his eyes, the endless blue of a cloudless summer sky.

Seemed a waste, to be honest.

"My lord." Honora bobbed politely, still holding on to Gideon. She was anxious to get the pleasantries over and have Huntly go somewhere else to lurk.

Huntly looked down on her from his great height. "Pleasure and all that, Mrs. Culpepper."

Honora raised a brow, taking in the giant of a man before her. The massive hands, drumming in boredom across one of his thighs, both of which were the size of a small tree trunks. The fact his waistcoat wasn't correctly buttoned. His cravat, which appeared to have been tied by a blind man. And he was rude.

Southwell had *terrible* taste in friends.

Huntly's gaze flicked over her bosom displayed to perfection in the gown.

A growl came from the back of Gideon's throat. "The card room is in the back, Hunt. Try not to insult anyone. I'm in no mood to stand as second for you in the morning."

Huntly immediately averted his eyes from Honora. "It's been ages since I've been in a duel. Besides, Montieth is a better second than you. I'll ask him if need be." Without another word, or even so much as a goodbye, Lord Huntly turned and lumbered across the room.

"Apologies, Honora." Gideon's gaze was on Huntly, who made his way through the throng of guests, carelessly stepping on one young lady's skirt. He didn't even pause or apologize when she cried out.

"So." She shifted back and forth. "He's lovely."

The dimple appeared in Gideon's cheek. "No, he isn't. Hunt is awful. If we weren't related, I might have allowed our relationship to fade away into the abyss of my past, much like Tarrington." He sighed. "He's not at all like Tarrington. I shouldn't joke about such a thing. But Hunt is often impolite. Rude. Poorly mannered. But for all that, he doesn't have a truly mean bone in his body. I tolerate him because he's family. You didn't come alone, did you?"

"No, my cousin, Emmagene, and I arrived together." She scanned the room for Emmie and only caught sight of Huntly tossing back a large glass of wine, spilling some of it on himself, much to the horror of those around him.

"Speaking of delightful relatives." Southwell squeezed her fingers.

The musicians struck up a waltz, the strains of the violins filling Lady Trent's ballroom. Honora's foot started to tap of its own accord, she being happy to watch from the wall, with

Gideon next to her. No matter what happened after tonight, she wanted to be with him. He was real for *her*. No matter what tomorrow would bring.

"Dance with me, Honora."

She looked over at him in surprise. "But you don't dance, my lord." Biting her lip, she nodded to his leg and lowered her voice. "You shouldn't, Gideon."

"I *can* dance. Possibly I don't glide about as well as I once did, but I have been practicing." His eyes caught hers. "I haven't wanted to dance with anyone else but you, Honora. And our last—that is to say, will you please do me the honor?" Gideon held out his hand.

Honora gazed into the face she'd both despised and adored since her first season, more beloved to her than any other. She clasped his fingers, struggling to keep the moisture from gathering in her eyes. "You don't have to do this. Not for me."

"I most assuredly do." He set his cane against the wall. "Don't let me forget that. You don't look strong enough to carry me to the carriage later. And I would appear quite unmanly if you did." Sweeping her into his arms, he pulled her close, moving stiffly and with much less agility than he once had.

Honora placed one hand on his shoulder, loving the way his hair brushed against her knuckles. The other hand, she placed very firmly on his chest, feeling the beat of his heart beneath her palm.

Southwell sucked in a lungful of air. "That's lovely. Don't stop doing that."

"Doing what?" She gave him a mischievous smile.

"Touching me." He spun her expertly, shuffling just a bit to keep his balance. "I've been waiting."

"I've touched you before now," she protested. Honora could recall every instant clearly. "Haven't you been paying attention?"

"Yes, but before, I was never sure you really wanted to." His nose lowered to nudge gently against her neck. "Now you do." The small bits of amber in his eyes glinted beneath the chandeliers. "I adore the dress, by the way. Very fetching. Though, I don't care for the admiration your bosom is drawing. I'm very possessive where you are concerned. As an only child, I never had to share anything, and I don't mean to start with you." There was a thread of steel in his words. "You should know that. If there are any objections to my wishing you all to myself, they should be voiced immediately."

"I had a feeling." The scent of him filled her nostrils. Cedar and leather. Maybe a hint of scotch. The smell, minus the scotch, reminded her of the small chest her grandmother had given Honora to store her most precious things. Poems. Books. She looked at Southwell.

My heart.

His hand, large and warm, splayed across her spine, the skirts of her gown wrapping about his legs as they danced. Gideon held her far too closely, their conversation appearing much too intimate. There would be no question of their relationship once this dance ended.

The fact Gideon was dancing at all sent shock waves through the other guests. Dozens of eyes watched him spin her about, including Emmie's.

Her cousin stood on the sidelines, disappointment clouding her sharp features.

"My lord," Honora whispered softly as the waltz faded. She was no longer at odds with her feelings over Southwell. And his for her. He'd very bluntly claimed her before half of London, dancing with her in his arms, though it pained him. Had very firmly told her, lest she suspect differently, that he had no intention of sharing her with anyone else.

"Will you take me home, my lord?" She swallowed. *"Your* home."

Gideon said nothing for so long Honora thought he might refuse her. Or call out that this had all been a game to him. Any moment, Tarrington would come barreling out, laughter on his florid face at putting one over on Miss Drevenport once again, and slap Gideon on the back.

None of that happened.

Gideon grabbed his cane but did not let go of her hand. She hoped he never would.

"Will we discuss Sebek?" he said quietly.

"Yes, my lord. I think a discussion of the Egyptian fertility god is much overdue." He knew her. He probably had for some time.

"Then yes. I want you home, Honora, with me."

He released her hand and offered his arm. Together they walked through Lady Trent's ballroom, uncaring what anyone thought or what would be said about them tomorrow.

The Duchess of Denby, ancient husband clutching her like a wild animal holds its prey, watched, jealousy spilling out from the misery coloring her features.

Tarrington, popping out from whatever rock he'd been hiding under, shot them both murderous looks from his place beside another rounded widow, at least ten years his senior.

Honora lifted her chin, tightening her hold on Gideon's arm. She was no longer interested in the past. Only the future.

CHAPTER THIRTEEN

I T HAD BEEN some time since Gideon had wished to have a woman in his bed. Not only had no one piqued his interest, but the scars twisting down the length of his leg and hip were the perfect excuse to avoid romantic entanglements. Even Anabeth, who claimed to love him madly and had been desperate to climb into bed with him, had looked askance at the destruction of the left side of his body. It was far easier to accomplish the same sort of release on his own, without pitying looks or pretending affection.

Ah, but his bloodthirsty Honora. He felt a great deal for her. Things that made him rethink his future.

He trailed his finger over her jaw as the carriage jostled them, bumping their bodies together. Pressing an openmouthed kiss to the elegant line of her neck, Gideon felt her pulse beating beneath his lips. Honora made the most delicious sounds when he touched her. Soft, feminine whimpers of arousal urging him further. Small squeaks begging him for more.

Gideon meant to explore every inch of *Miss Honora Drevenport* and enjoy the sounds she made as he did so.

He'd deliberately not asked to escort her to Lady Trent's tonight, stayed away from her since their museum outing, to give Honora time to consider, without his interference, what she would do.

So he'd waited by the wall until she'd spotted him tonight,

not knowing exactly how the evening would end. He certainly knew how Miss Stitch wanted things to go. Honora's cousin had circled the ballroom all evening like a vulture waiting until some poor animal expires, glaring daggers at Gideon whenever she'd caught sight of him.

Honora clung to him in the carriage, delicate hands running over his chest and shoulders.

"Gideon," she whispered, sliding her fingers inside his coat to trace the line of his ribs. His nose fell to her neck as his tongue leisurely traveled over the length of her shoulder. Cupping one breast, he pressed his thumb against the silk, rubbing back and forth until her nipple peaked, and a soft moan left her.

The carriage rolled to a stop before his town house. The steps of an approaching footman sounded on the stairs as Gideon quickly sought to untangle their limbs.

"Are you sure, Honora?"

"I am." She kissed him hard on the mouth.

Stepping out of the carriage and adjusting his coat, because his trousers had become unbelievably tight, he held out his hand to Honora.

Her fingers curled firmly around his, without hesitation.

CHAPTER FOURTEEN

"HONORA."

She turned from her perusal of the fireplace and the map hanging above it, a poorly drawn outline of the African continent. The coastline was all wrong...and rather lumpy.

"One of my first efforts."

Gideon stood before her, two glasses of what smelled like brandy in his hands, garbed only in his shirt and trousers. He'd discarded his cane downstairs, claiming he had no need of it for the rest of the evening. She supposed the remainder of his clothing had met the same fate and now lay somewhere in the dark corners of his massive bedroom, a space that looked part sleeping area and part work space. A wide table sat by the window, maps strewn across the top, along with a pile of pencils, a battered compass, and Spix's third volume on South America.

"A poor one at that," she said lightly, taking in the map.

"I was only twelve at the time," he said, half smile donning his lips. "I don't think it's all that bad."

"Africa isn't quite so lumpy, I'm sure. Nor is it egg-shaped."

"Horribly overeducated." His smile grew wider as he leaned in and touched his nose to hers.

His pale, white shirt hung open at the throat, showing a small swathe of the most perfect male skin and sprinkling of dark hair. "I've brought you a brandy." He held out one glass.

Honora gently sniffed at the rim. "I don't indulge in spirits often. Not until I met you, of course."

"Then sip slowly."

The firelight played along Southwell's lean form, creating lovely shadows across the elegantly sculpted bones of his face. "Beautiful creature," he whispered in her ear, pressing a kiss to her cheek.

"Not always," she replied a bit too harshly, thinking of the past. Mama had once told Honora that if Mama believed in changelings, Honora was certainly one. Marianne, Honora's sister, was slender and elegant, as was their mother. Nor was Marianne the least bookish. She painted watercolors of flowers and sang with a lovely voice. Had snagged a wealthy young baron and proceeded to produce a brood of well-behaved children while Honora remained childless and was likely barren.

"My mother would disagree with you most heartily, my lord." She took a large swallow of the brandy, struggling not to cough as it burned down her throat.

"I didn't mean only the way you look, Honora." He gently touched the space above her heart, which led to a caress along one of her breasts. Leaning over, he pressed a kiss to the spot where her nipple lay beneath the silk.

"Spoken like someone who has never felt unattractive or ugly." She gave him a sad smile. "You can't possibly understand what it's like to be judged by your physical appearance."

His hand fell from her breast, and he pulled away. As he tossed back the rest of the brandy, his face grew taut. Determined. He disappeared again to the far reaches of the room where she suspected either his valet lurked in a side room or there was some sort of antechamber where his clothes were kept. She returned her gaze to the flames, taking careful sips of the brandy.

She heard him pad back across the floor, felt his warmth as he stood behind her.

"Turn around." He sounded unbelievably angry at her. Pained in a way she'd never heard him before, not even when they'd talked about the black caiman. Or during their argument after the museum.

Honora turned. Blinked. Gideon had discarded what remained of his clothing. He was quite naked. And aroused. But that wasn't what made her stare. "Oh."

His eyes fluttered shut as if he couldn't bear to tolerate her perusal. "I think I do know what it is to feel ugly, Honora. Repulsive, even. I've literally had a woman scream at the sight of me."

Even in the firelight, the scars glowed a deep, ugly red. Terrible, twisted bits of skin and hair started just below his navel on the left side. Puncture marks pierced his thigh in a distinct pattern, one made by a caiman's mouth as it had tried to make a meal of Gideon. Three deep gouges started at his inner thigh and fell over his hip.

Claw marks.

And his leg—his poor, battered left leg—looked as if the skin had been partially peeled off. Torn. *Shredded.* A soft gasp left her. Not for the horror before her but the agony Gideon had to have endured. The sheer terror he must have experienced.

His eyes remained tightly shut. "I realize it isn't exactly the same, *Miss Drevenport*. But I do think I have some experience at being judged for my appearance. The first woman who saw me naked after it happened almost fainted." His eyes snapped open. "And the second. I didn't care to try to fuck anyone after that."

"Gideon—" Her hand trembled, nearly causing her to spill the brandy.

"So I will understand, *Miss Drevenport*, if you wish to leave. Perhaps it will give you some sense of justification for any wrong committed against you. You may also say I can't perform as a man, if you wish, though I think we both know"—he gestured to his cock jutting from between his thighs—"that would be a lie."

A tear slid down her cheek, and she brushed it away, spilling brandy on herself. She set the glass down before cupping his face between her hands. "I don't wish to leave you."

Not ever.

"How long have you known?" she whispered.

"Since I saw you in that crimson dress." His gaze on her was heated. "But you weren't ready to tell me or didn't want to. You needed to prove something to yourself and possibly me as well. I give you permission, Honora, should you need to prove your point, as you did with Tarrington"—his words grew thick—"if it will ease you."

"I don't need to, Gideon. I promise." Bringing his mouth to hers, Honora tried to convey the depth of feeling for him.

Love. That's what I feel for Gideon.

His arms came around her, embracing her so hard Honora thought her ribs would crack. Gideon kissed her back fiercely. Urgently. As if he'd been starved for her his entire life. Tearing his mouth from hers, he spun her around, attacking the back of her gown, the delicate satin buttons torn off in his haste.

Honora watched in utter fascination as one rolled under the bed. She'd never be able to retrieve it and have it resewn. She arched her back, turning her chin up to view him. "Am I being ravished?"

"Not quite yet." Mouth hot against her neck, Gideon tugged and pulled until Honora was left in only her chemise and the armor of her corset.

"God*damn* it." Limping over to the bookcase, Gideon muttered about the difficulty of women's clothing as he pushed aside a stack of books, uncaring when they tumbled to the floor. Finally he spun back to her with a wicked smile, a small knife in one hand.

"No, Gideon. Wait." Honora held up her palm. She'd never get her dress back on again without the corset. Bad enough it wouldn't completely button.

"I hate these things." He pointed at the corset. "Is this why you're faint half the time and won't eat?" He approached her as a hunter does his prey. Raising the knife, he deftly sliced through the strings of her corset.

Honora took a deep gulp of air, looking down in dismay at the remains of *the* most important item of her wardrobe. "It's necessary for dresses to fit properly. I'm...*rounded.*"

"*Delightfully curved* is the phrase you're looking for. I happen to adore every inch of you. And I can't believe you punish yourself in such a way."

He tore at her chemise as she unsuccessfully tried to push his fingers away.

"You'll tear it," she pleaded, though she was secretly enjoying how desperate he was to have her.

"Excellent idea." Gideon ripped the garment down the front.

Honora made a sigh of distress, wondering how in the world she could return home without a corset and with a torn chemise and a dress missing half its buttons.

"Don't worry." He nipped at her bottom lip. "I'll buy you another. Dozens. Red, I think. I adore you in red." A big hand cupped her breast, gently rolling the nipple between his forefinger and thumb. "Take down your hair, *Miss Drevenport.*"

"You were the only one who ever addressed me correctly. Did you know that?"

"I know." He paused and kissed her tenderly. "Now take down your bloody hair."

Taking a step back, Gideon surveyed her, a large, predatory male, the horrible scars giving him a dangerous, otherworldly look. He was an angry god, perhaps. Or some mythical creature. Her gaze trailed over the graceful curvatures of muscle in his shoulders and arms, all brushed with dark hair. The sharp lines of his hips, the left still discernible beneath the scars.

Lowering her eyes, Honora pulled the pins struggling to hold back the unruly mass of her hair, her fingers stilling as she looked, *really looked*, at Gideon's...*cock.*

Oh dear. Culpepper had been deficient in more ways than one. "No wonder Anabeth popped out at you in her under-things." She kicked off her slippers before bending to take off her stockings, using her hair to shield the curves of her body.

"No," he growled. "Leave them on." Gideon took a backward step toward the bed and held out his hand. "Come here to me."

"Might we dim the lamp?" It was rather daunting to stand here before him, all her curves on display, with only her hair as protection.

"No, we may not. I want to see all of you. As you have seen all of me. Don't you believe in fairness, sweetheart? Besides, you're bloody gorgeous."

"I am always fair." Honora took a deep breath and shook out her hair, delighting in the way Gideon watched the heavy black curls fall over her shoulders. She had never felt so beautiful, so wanted, in all her life. Coming forward, she gasped as his hand splayed possessively across her stomach before he cupped her mound.

Gideon's fingers tangled in the soft hair before sliding into her already damp flesh, eyes never leaving hers.

"I want you desperately, Miss Drevenport. More than I've ever wanted anything. Not even an undiscovered city in a South American jungle could tempt me half as much. Do you believe me?"

Only Gideon would compare making love to her as slightly more intriguing than a pile of ancient stone. But she took his point. "Yes." She fell back against the bed and shut her eyes, waiting to feel Gideon's weight fall upon her. Culpepper had always made her lie flat to accept his attentions.

Nothing happened. She opened her eyes an inch.

Gideon was watching her, the dimple deepening in his cheek. He lowered his head, pressing a kiss to the small bulge of her stomach. His tongue traced a reddened line left behind from her stays. He nibbled up another red streak beneath her ribs. "Have your dresses let out," he murmured against her skin. "I want you to eat tarts with me."

"That isn't—what I mean to say—" Honora found it difficult to concentrate, especially after he sucked one of her nipples into the heat of his mouth.

His tongue circled before his teeth grazed the taut peak. "You've lovely breasts, Honora. Good God, they're amazing."

"Thank you," she moaned as he trailed his mouth back down to her stomach, licking and sucking at her skin. She ran her hands over his shoulders, feeling the slide of his muscles beneath the tips of her fingers. It was only when she registered a puff of air against her bared flesh that her eyes opened again.

"What are you doing?" She sat up to see his dark hair between her thighs, dangerously close to...well, a very private part of herself.

"Just a kiss, Honora." His eyes were dark. Hooded. Gideon's tongue flicked out. "I want to taste you. I meant to do this the day of our picnic."

She gulped for air. "Your leg," she stuttered. "And—" The remainder of her thought was cut off by the sinuous movement of his tongue, lapping and teasing at her flesh.

Gideon roughly pushed her thighs apart, hooking one leg over his shoulder.

Honora didn't object. Couldn't possibly make even a sound of protest. She was too busy whispering his name as pleasure moved across her body, all of it emanating from the press of Gideon's mouth against her. The sensations sharpened, honed to a brilliant edge by his tongue, as he lapped at the small bud hidden within her folds. He deliberately teased, leaving her to writhe before him on the bed, begging him. Her hands slapped at his shoulders and clutched at his hair.

Ever so slowly, he eased two fingers inside her channel, curling the tips slightly to massage a sensitive spot within her as he gently sucked the small, sensitive bit of flesh more fully into his mouth.

Honora's hips shot off the bed. "Gideon." Her back arched, chin tipping toward the ceiling as the most exquisite sensations rippled down her limbs. She closed her eyes as waves of pleasure rolled over her, her fingers tangling in Gideon's hair. When the last of the tremors began to fade, Honora finally opened her eyes to find Gideon watching her.

His eyes were narrowed. Predatory. As if he wished to conquer her.

"I didn't realize how marvelous that could be," she breathed, the sight of his head between her splayed thighs incredibly erotic.

"I'm far from done," he growled, kissing his way back up her body to nibble at the taut peaks of her breasts. When he finally reached her mouth, she sighed, parting her lips with little urging, tasting herself and brandy on his tongue. Their mouths moved in tandem as Gideon's hands explored the curves and hollows of her body, dipping every so often back between her legs.

Honora explored as well, her palms flattening over the sculpted lines of his back and buttocks, inciting Gideon to make the most curious sounds. When her fingers moved to his left hip, however, she felt him tense.

Carefully, she ran her forefinger along the line of one ugly, raised scar. Honora wished she could press her mouth to the twisted skin. Kiss him tenderly. She unfolded her hand, caressing him with a light, delicate touch.

"Gideon," she murmured against his lips.

He turned his head, pressing a kiss to her palm. "No one else." He nipped at her wrist. "I wasn't joking about that."

"I didn't expect you were, my lord."

Gideon brought her hands above her head, lacing his fingers with hers, entering her carefully, giving her time to adjust. He never looked away but pressed his forehead to hers, the truth of his feelings stamped clearly across his handsome features.

"*This* is forever, Honora." He pulled back before thrusting so deep inside her she gave a small cry. As he rocked his hips against hers, Honora's last thought before becoming completely immersed in the pleasure between them was that he was right.

She and Gideon had always been bound together.

CHAPTER FIFTEEN

THE FIRE CRACKLED and popped, sending sparks against the hearth as a log fell into the grate. A slice of moonlight shone through the window, bathing Gideon in silver light as Honora ran her fingers over the line of his ribs. She lay on her side, her smaller body partially draped over his, the wild mass of her hair tangled around them both. The steady thud of his heart sounded beneath her ear.

Honora was so *bloody* happy.

"Would you like to go to Egypt with me one day?" Gideon wrapped a length of her hair around his thumb. "I'll teach you how to ride a camel. Take you down the Nile, where you will *not* be attacked by a hippo. We'll speak of Sebek."

Honora lowered her gaze. "We don't need to talk about...before."

"Yes, we do, Honora. There is no sense in avoiding it." A puff of air—due to frustration, she thought—came from between his lips. "I make no excuse for my poor behavior in accepting a wager to dance with the most unattractive girl Anabeth could find."

She pushed away from him, suddenly not wishing to hear anything further. It was painful for her to relive that night. Remember the pathetic creature she'd once been, one who'd readily been manipulated into marrying Culpepper because she'd been so devastated.

"I know all about Tarrington's wager. You were so horrified

at me, poor, lovesick creature that I was, you feared I might follow you about in an attempt to be compromised." Her voice raised an octave. "So you fled London as soon as possible to avoid such an unwelcome instance." She pushed against his chest. "While I was left with no other option but to marry Culpepper, who cared not a fig for me, only my father's copper mines."

He pulled her roughly against his chest. "I was thoughtless. Arrogant. I accepted a wager to dance with the most unattractive girl Anabeth could bring me, yes. But she brought *you*. A young lady I *did not* find repulsive in the least."

"You don't have to say that given—"

"I've spent most of the night between your thighs?"

She shrugged and became immersed in the pattern of dark hair on his chest.

"I was only supposed to dance with you," he continued in a quiet tone. "That was the wager. Not indulge in a spirited discussion with the most interesting young lady I'd ever met. One I didn't find nearly as unappealing to me as Anabeth assumed. I was under no obligation to bring you out on the terrace once the dance ended. My journey to South America had already been planned, and leaving had nothing to do with you despite the rumors Tarrington spread." He pressed a kiss to the top of her head. "I nearly kissed you that night."

"Because I was so beautiful?" She snorted derisively.

"No," he replied honestly. "You were awkward and uncomfortable in your own skin. Your hair was a mess. But I—did you not feel it? When we danced that night? I honestly don't know what would have happened if I'd stayed in England."

Honora took a deep breath. "Please don't lie. There isn't any reason to." It was far easier, especially at this moment, for her to pretend she'd never been Miss Drevenport.

"I'm not lying to you. What bloody reason would I have to do so now? I've already seduced you."

"The seduction was mutual, but very well, I see your point," she said grudgingly.

"I was ashamed of what had happened, but I did not try to make things right, though I'm not sure what I could have done at that point but beat Tarrington senseless. But what you did to him was far more fitting." A sigh escaped him. "I never forgot *you*, Honora. Not your intelligence or your bloodthirsty nature. The image of you that night faded in time; all that came to mind was a wild, barely constrained tangle of fuzzy hair, and eyes the color of jade. But when I saw you again—" His finger trailed down her cheek. "As beautiful as the Widow Culpepper looked in that crimson gown, it was Miss Drevenport I wanted. I remembered how you made me feel, here." His hand pressed to his heart. "I know it doesn't make sense."

Honora did understand. It was why the scars he bore didn't bother her in the least. Why she'd never been able to forget Gideon, no matter how hard she'd tried. "Is this the end of your groveling?"

"No. It will continue for some time. Years, probably. Much of it will be done naked." He gently rubbed his nose to hers. "At least now I know why I survived the black caiman, why even when the pain was so fierce I wished to die and just be left to rot in the jungle, I struggled to live."

"Why?" She smiled against his chest.

"For you. For this. It is worth any price I had to pay."

Honora held his gaze, wishing she could see, despite how the room wasn't bright enough, the sparkle of amber in his eyes. There were so many things she adored about him. The high cheekbones, the tiny scar beneath one ear that she still hadn't inquired about, the brush of dark hair along his jaw. His sense of adventure. His brilliance.

But it was his *heart* Honora loved most of all.

"I forgive you, Gideon Lawrence, Earl of Southwell. For Tarrington. Culpepper. All of it."

CHAPTER SIXTEEN

G IDEON'S CARRIAGE ROLLED through the quiet streets of London just as the sky was turning pink. It would be dawn soon. Honora looked up at the house she shared with her mother-in-law, though she would not do so for much longer. Having decided earlier to vacate the premises and forever close the Culpepper chapter of her life, now she had more incentive to do so. Her own home, where she could be as indiscreet with Gideon as she wished, would suit her better.

Gideon had made it very clear to Honora, as he'd taken her roughly this morning when she'd been barely awake, that the Widow Culpepper was no longer on the market, so to speak.

Honora smiled to herself. She adored possessive Gideon.

She'd managed to deter him from the insistence he see her home. Bad enough Honora was arriving before the sun was fully up, in a strange carriage. The sight would practically announce she'd spent the night with a lover. If her neighbors caught sight of Gideon, the gossip would be enormous.

He'd grumbled but had given in to her.

Honora, for her part, had some things she needed to make clear to Gideon as well. The first being that the Widow Culpepper, despite the gossip, had never taken any other man to her bed save the Earl of Southwell, and Culpepper, of course. She hadn't felt as if it needed to be said, as surely Gideon could tell Honora wasn't...*experienced*, so to speak. But in the spirit of starting fresh with each other, she meant to be honest when she saw him again.

Gideon had promised, as he'd bid her goodbye with a kiss on the tip of her nose, that he would send a note later. They would talk more. Dine together if she wished. There was a lovely map he wanted her to see, but it must be looked at while they were both naked.

Humming to herself, Honora clutched the cloak he'd lent her, burrowing deep inside as much to hide her disheveled appearance as to revel in Gideon's scent. It was early enough that Loretta and, indeed, most of the household, would still be abed.

One of the young footmen opened the door, rubbing sleep from his eyes. He offered to take the cloak, so tired he didn't so much as blink at her attire, but Honora waved him off. She yawned and quietly made her way up the stairs.

Reaching the safety of her room, Honora shut the door behind her, unable to stop her face from splitting into a grin. Happiness, the kind that suffused you from inside out, filled her. She danced like an idiot around her bed.

Nothing could ruin this day. She simply wouldn't allow it.

MUCH LATER, AFTER having a bath and sleeping nearly until it was time for tea, Honora moved quietly down the hall, not wishing to alert Loretta to her presence. The less time she spent in her mother-in-law's company, the better. She didn't wish to be drawn into their usual pattern of hurled insults and anger. Honora was far too joyful. A note from Gideon was probably waiting for her in the silver tray by the door.

As she passed the drawing room, Honora caught the scent of freshly baked scones. Her stomach growled, stating the toast, tea, and poached egg she'd had while waiting for her bath hadn't been nearly enough after the previous night's activities.

"Harlot," Loretta hissed from the depths of the drawing

room, catching sight of Honora. "Still sneaking about, I see."

Honora searched for one drop of kindness to douse her rising irritation toward her mother-in-law. She conceded that their current contentious relationship was not wholly Loretta's fault. Striding into the room, Honora faced the spiteful old woman before her, determined to be polite.

"Good afternoon, Loretta."

"Scheming whore."

Honora steeled her resolve. "I can see you're in a pleasant mood today. Shall I ring for a maid to help you to your room?" Honora snatched a scone from the tray and calmly poured herself some tea. Now would be the time to confess her lovers had all been imaginary, conjured up solely to annoy her mother-in-law, but she doubted Loretta would believe her. She would give Loretta this house, explain her own actions in lying about having a horde of beaux, and move on from all things Culpepper.

With Gideon.

"You'll grow fat again." Loretta followed the movement of the scone into Honora's mouth.

"That isn't your concern." Honora nibbled on the scone.

"You know what is my concern, Honora? The Culpepper family name. Which I will no longer allow you to disgrace. I won't have you in this house, sullying my family and my son's memory. Prostituting yourself with any man who pays you the least bit of attention. I know everything you've done."

There was another teacup, half-full, sitting on the table before Loretta's. An empty plate filled with crumbs sat off to the side. A sign Loretta had had a caller while Honora had slept away part of the day.

"I haven't actually done anything." Loretta must be listening to the tales being peddled about Honora by Tarrington. He'd been spewing gossip regarding her since her dismissal of him in full view of every guest at the Pemberton ball. Taking a small bite of the scone, she said, "There are things we need to discuss. Things you should know."

"I agree." An ugly smirk widened Loretta's mouth, showing a row of yellowed teeth. "Allow me to start. My son was much too good for you, but he wanted your father's copper mines. He was to get a child in you, possibly more than one. Then we were going to have you put away due to your fragile state. Locked away for your own safety. I planned on telling everyone you were a danger to yourself and others."

The scone tasted like dust in Honora's mouth. "No one would have believed that."

"Your mother did, as did the rest of your family. They believed every word I said. Especially after your delicate sensibilities wouldn't allow guests."

Honora tried to swallow the bit of pastry stuck in her throat and found she could not. "My cousin Emmagene would never have believed you or allowed you to send me away."

"Yes. Miss Stitch. Horrid girl. Speaks very loudly. Easy to overhear."

"You've been eavesdropping when she visits?"

Loretta only smiled. "I always thought you pathetic. Good Lord, you were so unattractive the first time I caught sight of you I wondered what Dalward was thinking."

"Not so now," Honora snapped.

"At the very least, I thought you could provide a child or two. Dalward was disgusted by you. That never changed. But he knew his duty to provide an heir. *Barren.*" She hissed the word. "Your womb is as putrid as the rest of you."

Honora clenched her fists, the first stirrings of panic making her heart beat wildly within her chest. How much had her mother-in-law overheard during Emmie's visits? Too much. Likely everything Honora had planned for Tarrington.

And Southwell.

"Woodridge, Belmont. Tarrington. *Montieth,*" she spat. "Destroying gentlemen for your own amusement. I heard all about what you did to poor Tarrington after seducing him, you strumpet. Now Southwell, a fine gentleman of great renown, is in your clutches. You entertained Belmont only moments before leaving for Lady Trent's ball."

"That isn't true." Honora's lovers had *all* been imaginary. And because they'd been made up, she'd never once mentioned anyone's name to Loretta.

Yes, but someone has.

"Revenge for some imagined slight he did you years ago." She nodded triumphantly to Honora. "Oh yes. I know all about that now. My poor Dalward. Induced to offer for you out of pity."

"And copper mines," Honora said sharply.

"Southwell must hate joining a game of cards, never knowing if the gentleman he's sitting across from has bedded you." She picked up her tea, shooting Honora a satisfied glance over the rim. "But he does now. I've made sure of it, you scheming strumpet."

Honora once again glanced to the empty plate and teacup sitting on the table. She'd been so certain that nothing and no one could destroy her happiness with Gideon.

Except this horrid old woman could. And probably Lord Tarrington.

"Get out of my house." Loretta thumped her hand so hard on the table one of the plates fell to the floor.

Loretta had never shown Honora any kindness. Had offered no comfort. The fact that her son had taken advantage of Honora after what Tarrington had done was reprehensible but, in Loretta's mind, somehow justified. They'd meant to lock her away, and her parents would have allowed them to.

"I'll be writing to Winifred today." Honora stood and strode to the door, unease over Gideon gnawing away at her.

"Why?" Loretta pulled her black skirts around her, like a bat wrapping its wings.

"Because I've decided to sell this house and everything in it. You've reminded me there are no fond memories to keep me here." Honora watched as Loretta sputtered. "I'd hate for you to be put out on the street."

The howl that met her ears, like something evil being put to rest, echoed loudly in the drawing room until Honora shut the door behind her.

CHAPTER SEVENTEEN

HONORA WALKED SWIFTLY about the garden, making a neat circle among the trees. She'd sent a note to Gideon immediately after the heated discussion with Loretta and received only a blunt, vague response from his secretary that he was busy with estate business but would call on her soon.

That had been two days ago.

One, two, three, four. It took seven paces to circle the weeping willow.

At first, Honora wanted to believe it was merely business that kept Gideon from her, but as time dragged on, she was forced to face the fact that he wasn't going to call. Or send her a note. Anxious and worried, she'd almost convinced herself she was the victim of yet another prank. One in which Tarrington had exacted revenge by using Southwell.

Footsteps echoed on the stone path, and Honora looked up, hoping it was Gideon, but it was only Emmie, garbed in her usual dark colors, stomping toward Honora. It felt like a lifetime since she'd accompanied her cousin to Lady Trent's ball, instead of only a few days. "Emmie."

"Thought I was someone else, perhaps?"

Honora nodded. "Hoping." She gave her cousin an apologetic smile. "I am glad to see you regardless."

Her cousin's face was pinched. Worried. "You won't be happy after I tell you why I'm here. I've just had a visit from your mother, an experience that is never welcome. She has to be the most desperate of creatures to seek me out."

Honora's mother disliked Emmie, though she was her niece. This could in no way be good.

"She interrogated me," Emmie bit out, "for nearly an hour on your scores of lovers, wanting to know if I helped you arrange your indiscretions, including the one you supposedly had in the carriage on the way to Lady Trent's ball."

"You were the only other person in that carriage." Honora shook her head. "What tripe. I don't have scores of lovers."

I have one. Just one. Her heart constricted painfully at the thought of Gideon.

"Your pretend lovers, all of whom have been named, are not denying the association. One claims to be the gentleman in the carriage." Emmie rolled her eyes. "She didn't tell me which one."

This is very bad. If Honora's mother assumed she was entertaining dozens of lovers, it meant all of London did as well. Gideon would hear the gossip and be hurt by it.

"I'm to inform you that your parents will not receive you. Nor will Marianne. Can't imagine you're too distraught about that. Your sister is such a righteous little prig. She sat by your mother and twittered that she always imagined you'd come to a bad end one day."

The family's rejection of her still stung even now that she knew they would have allowed Culpepper to put her away.

"There's more." Emmie flushed, something she never did, which sent Honora's stomach roiling. "Our discussion about the disparagement of Southwell and his injuries—" She bit her lip. "Well, your mother knew what was said, Honora. I don't see how she could, but—" Emmie opened her hands before clutching them again into fists. "Your lover, the night of Lady Trent's ball—"

"I had no lover that night save Gideon."

Emmie's cheeks pinked again. "—claims you mentioned to him how you meant to discard Southwell because of his inability to satisfy you."

"How could anyone believe such nonsense? Can't everyone see that Tarrington is behind this attack on my character because I refused the offer to become his mistress? These other 'lovers' are in league with Tarrington. They have to be. And as far as my conversation with you, Emmie, Loretta overheard us. About what I did to Tarrington. What you assumed I meant to do to Southwell."

"That's rather unfortunate. She's probably told everyone who will listen."

"I am resolved to call on Gideon this afternoon." Honora paused as another wave of doubt filled her. Surely he wouldn't believe Loretta over her. "He has been busy with estate business, and I didn't want to bother him, but I need to make him aware of what's happened."

"You don't know." Emmie gave her a confused look. "Honora, he's gone. Southwell. He's left you. He's no longer in town."

"No. He wouldn't leave London without telling me." Honora didn't even sound convincing to her own ears.

"Southwell has abandoned you to the wolves. As he did before. Just as I warned you he would do."

"Where is he?" Honora demanded. "It isn't as if he can conveniently join an expedition this time, not with his leg. And he hasn't abandoned me, Emmie." At least Honora didn't really think he had.

Emmie shrugged. "It is my understanding he has fled to his country estate. Because of the"—she looked upward, almost as if she didn't wish to say the word—"humiliation you've dealt him. At least, according to the gossips."

Honora wobbled, ever so slightly. He really did believe the worst of her.

How could he?

"So let me understand, Emmie." Honora started to pace back and forth. "The man I love has been convinced of my numerous affairs, including one I had with his best friend, Lord Montieth, and a gentleman who I was apparently indiscreet with in a carriage. After which I spent the night with *him*. He believes that I am planning on discarding him and intend to tell everyone in London he is unable to bed me because of injuries he suffered previously. Which is ridiculous. I'm still sore."

"At least"—Emmie looked chagrined—"according to gossip."

Honora had never been more furious or hurt in her life. And that included what Tarrington had done to her when she'd been Miss Drevenport. "I love Gideon, Emmie."

"I *know* that." Her cousin's sharp features softened. "But does *he* realize that? Did you tell him? Why would he believe these rumors without even talking to you?"

A vision of Gideon, standing naked before her, firelight illuminating the horror of the left side of his body, flashed before Honora's eyes. The horrible, ruined lines of Gideon's hip and thigh. The other women who'd found him repulsive. How he'd told her he had been expecting the same treatment as she'd dealt Tarrington. "Someone convinced him. I doubt it was Tarrington or Loretta."

Emmie took her hand. "I'm so sorry, Honora. I had no idea Loretta overheard our conversation, else I would never have spoken. As much as I dislike Southwell, I would never hurt you in such a way. Please believe me."

"I do." Honora's mind sifted through the last discussion she'd had with Loretta. "I'm certain Tarrington has been here." Honora spun on her heel and walked rapidly back into the house. "Loretta had a visitor the day after Lady Trent's ball. She rarely has callers. I thought it odd at the time. I want to know who it was."

Honora stood in the foyer. "Edward," she called out for the butler, who appeared magically as if he'd been hiding in the paneling of the wall, just waiting for her summons. "I have something to ask you and I would appreciate the truth."

"Of course, madam." His eyes flicked to Emmie, who stood, arms crossed, ready to do battle.

"The day after Lady Trent's ball, Mrs. Culpepper was sitting in the drawing room, having tea but not by herself. Who came to call?"

"I'm not sure—"

"Edward," Honora said pointedly. "Mrs. Culpepper doesn't receive many visitors these days. Hardly anyone calls. There is no possible way you don't know who visited her. And I'll kindly remind you it is my house you preside over."

His face reddened at the rebuke. "Lord Tarrington."

Honora nodded. She'd assumed as much. Her and Gideon's bumping into Tarrington at the museum hadn't been accidental. He'd probably been planning on hurting Honora and Gideon since. So Tarrington had given Loretta, who'd likely cackled with malicious pleasure at how right she'd been about her daughter-in-law, the names of Honora's so-called lovers. Loretta had probably told Tarrington about what she'd overheard right before Honora had left for Lady Trent's ball.

Lady Trent. "That's who he would believe."

"Who?" Emmie shot her a confused look.

"Lady Trent. Montieth's mother." How had Honora not thought of her before? Gideon had said Lady Trent was like a mother to him. He'd mentioned their close relationship more than once. Loretta must have written to her. For all Honora knew, they'd been corresponding this entire time. Long enough for Loretta to spill her vitriol all over Lady Trent and convince her of Honora's deceit.

"One more question, Edward. Did a letter go out to Lady Trent shortly after Lord Tarrington's visit?"

He bowed. "I sent the messenger myself."

"Thank you, Edward." Honora waved him away and turned to her cousin. "He would believe Lady Trent if she came to him with such damning evidence against me. I wish I could say he would not, but—" Honora twisted her fingers together, thinking of Gideon in the firelight, waiting for her to push him away in disgust.

"What will you do?" Emmie asked.

Honora's first inclination was to allow Gideon to stew. He'd left her, believing Lady Trent without even speaking to Honora or allowing her to explain. It meant he didn't trust her or their connection. It pained her terribly, but part of Honora understood. What she could not do was allow the misunderstanding to fester between them.

"I'm going after him," Honora stated firmly. "Today."

"But you don't know where his country estate is, Honora. I haven't any idea either. I suppose we can ask"—her lip curled—"my brother's wife, Rebecca. But I'm not sure she knows."

"Which is why I'm going to pay a call to the Earl of Montieth. I do hope Lady Trent is visiting, because I would like a few words with her. Edward," she called into the seemingly deserted hallway. "Have the carriage brought around. I'm going out."

CHAPTER EIGHTEEN

ALMOST EVERYONE KNEW where the Earl of Montieth lived. His family was so ancient and prestigious they'd managed to snag a plot of land in a very desirable location, one they'd held on to for several generations. Made of white brick, with ivy crawling up one side, Montieth's London home was tucked into a small pocket next to the park. It was fairly easy to find.

He wasn't pleased to receive Honora, but he did.

"I'm sure I'd remember," Montieth drawled in his snide, arrogant way as he greeted her, "if you and I had been indiscreet, Mrs. Culpepper."

"I would have had to be foxed," Honora replied. "So completely filled with spirits as to not recall my own name. Did you inform your mother of such? I'm sure she's visited."

"I had the delight of first being accused of a crime I didn't commit—namely, bedding you beneath my friend's nose, madam. Which I staunchly denied. I then had the pleasure of being informed of all your trespasses. The evidence against you is much more damning, Mrs. Culpepper. Were you really going to tell everyone he couldn't bed you because a caiman nearly took his leg off? All over some incident that happened when you were a girl?" Montieth let out growl of anger toward her. "You and your bitch of a cousin have much to answer for."

Honora took a step forward. "If your involvement with me was lied about, my lord, why are you so certain the remainder is the truth?"

Montieth glared at her for the longest time before taking a piece of paper from his desk and scribbling out instructions to Southwell's estate, Longwood. At least, she hoped the directions were to Longwood. Montieth could be sending her on a wild goose chase for all she knew. He held the paper out to her.

Honora's fingers closed over the edge of the note, but Montieth didn't let go immediately. He tugged until she had to lean forward.

"Don't break him again, Mrs. Culpepper. I'll be rather put out if you do."

Honora gave him a brittle smile, snatching the paper from his fingers. Montieth could threaten all he wished. She didn't feel the need to grant him any reassurances, imposing brute that he was. She didn't give a fig for his opinion. Or him.

Several hours later, Honora looked out at the gently rolling hills outside the coach window. She'd been along this road before. It was the same direction she and Gideon had traveled for their picnic. His estate wasn't so far from London at all, it seemed.

The sun began to set as Longwood came into view. Admiring the tall columns and arched roof, Honora tried not to worry over what would happen if Gideon chose not to listen to her. Or had decided she wasn't worth the trouble.

The irony was she'd accomplished her long-ago scheme to break Gideon's heart only to find out how terrible it really was.

The coach rolled to a stop before the door as two footman and a butler came to greet her, looking askance at Honora and the coach bearing a small mountain of trunks.

The butler, a bulky man with suspicious eyes, gave her a pointed look, trying to maintain a polite demeanor. He had a scar just below one cheek and a nose that had been broken. Very uncommon-looking for a butler. She wondered where Gideon had found him.

Bowing slightly, the butler raised a brow. "I am Dunst. This is the home of the Earl of Southwell." He looked again at her coach, devoid of any family crest. "May I be of assistance?"

"Yes, you may." Honora bestowed a brilliant smile on him. "I wish to see Lord Southwell. I am Mrs. Culpepper," she supplied, waiting for any sort of reaction from the butler. Finding none, she soldiered on. "He isn't expecting me."

The butler was eyeing Honora as if she was...*well*, some sort of light-skirts. "Lord Southwell is not receiving. Nor is he in need of your services, madam. There is an inn a short distance away. Perhaps you can avail yourself—"

Honora marched right past Dunst, ignoring his attempts to stop her, and strode into the foyer. If she was going to be thrown out, the butler and shocked footmen would have to bodily pick her up and toss her into the coach. She wasn't leaving until she spoke to Gideon.

"Gideon!" Honora shouted, listening to her voice echo over the tiled entry.

Dunst was at her heels. "Madam. I must ask you to leave. Immediately." The butler's polite accent had dropped. He sounded like he belonged on the docks. Which was probably where Gideon had found him.

"Did you travel with Lord Southwell, perhaps? Maybe went down the Amazon with him? Never mind." She waved him away as if he was nothing more than a gnat. "Where's the study? No, better, where is the room in which Lord Southwell drinks and makes maps?"

Dunst didn't answer, but his gaze flickered down the hall. He reached for her arm. The butler was large. Muscular. But he wasn't agile in the least. She had no trouble ducking around him to dash down the hall, which was difficult considering how tightly she was laced. Wouldn't it be disappointing if she came all this way only to faint?

A door at the end of the hall stood open. Ink, cedar, and scotch fumes floated to her. The room reeked of them. She imagined the man sitting before the fire did as well.

CHAPTER NINETEEN

"CHRIST." GIDEON ROLLED his head toward the door, which made the room spin just a bit but not so much that he couldn't see the petite form of a woman storming into his study. There was no mistaking all those delicious curves.

"Go away, Miss Drevenport." The very sight of her made his chest hurt. "If you've come to gloat, please do so from where you are. Once you are finished, leave."

Dunst appeared behind her in the doorway. He looked ready to toss her out on her lovely, plump ass. "I'm sorry, my lord. She slipped by me."

Gideon gave a wave, which made him nearly spill his drink. "It isn't your fault, Dunst. Miss Drevenport is far more devious than she'd have you believe."

"The lady says her name is Mrs. Culpepper." Dunst's broad forehead wrinkled.

"I'm both, Dunst. Please shut the door behind you. I'll ring if you're needed."

Dunst looked askance at her, uncertain whether to obey.

"It's all right, Dunst." Gideon waved again, uncaring when the scotch spilled on his arm. His bloody leg hurt terribly, along with the rest of him. He had to admire her determination to eviscerate him after spending the night with him. He'd even told her she should, if it would ease some of the wound he'd given her so long ago. Now *he* was the laughingstock of London. Not that he cared what that group of prigs and staunch matrons thought, but—

"I'm so *bloody* angry at you right now, Gideon." She stamped her foot.

Miss Drevenport was really a tiny thing. Rounded in all the proper ways. Like a porcelain doll. Smart as a whip. He was madly in love with her, a thought that was very unwelcome just now.

"I haven't done anything. At least this time." He took another sip of his scotch, barely tasting it. "Your anger is misplaced."

"You left without even talking to me first."

"Was it necessary? I did tell you to disparage me if, in doing so, it brought you happiness. Did it bring you happiness, Miss Drevenport?"

"Do I look happy, Gideon?"

No, she didn't. He hoped there wasn't anything sharp lying around, but Miss Drevenport would more likely throw a book. She loved books.

He'd stayed drunk since leaving London, and it took him a moment to recall what, exactly, had happened. Lady Trent, whom he adored, had visited him, a tear running down her cheek as she'd held out a letter from Loretta Culpepper. It was terrible, what had been written there. And there were more letters. Details of conversations Loretta Culpepper had overheard. Names of Honora's lovers. He felt like an idiot. He'd been so certain *he'd* been her only lover.

"Lady Trent brought me a note—several, actually—from your mother-in-law."

Miss Drevenport made a terrible face.

"*The* Mrs. Culpepper was quite descriptive. But some of her words held a ring of truth. Still, I escorted out Lady Trent and put the letter aside, and I went to White's, deciding whether I would confront Montieth over the possibility of his being your lover." He tried to focus on her face. "He never gave me a straight answer, you see, at Lady Pemberton's ball, when you and I were reintroduced."

"Oh, Gideon." Her eyes fluttered shut.

"Belmont found me and took me aside." He tried to give her a pointed look, but she was much too blurry. "*Belmont*," he said again, "who appraised me he'd had you shortly before we consummated—" He paused, feeling the way his heart squeezed. "I forgot how bloodthirsty you are, Miss Drevenport."

"I don't even know Lord Belmont." She sounded angry.

"He claims to know you very well." Gideon's fingers tightened over the glass. "And he isn't a lord, just a mister. Why don't you know that?"

"Possibly because I've never met the man." She placed her hands on her hips and stared him down. "I've been told I'm highly intelligent—by you, as a matter of fact—several times. Surely if I were tupping him, I wouldn't have missed how to address him properly. Can you not see that Tarrington put him up to it? All of them? Even Loretta?"

"Lady Trent—"

"—has been manipulated as well. How could you believe I would hurt you even if Lady Trent was presenting the evidence?" She came down on her knees before the chair, which gave him a lovely view of her bosom. He unfurled his fingers, just thinking about those delicious mounds in his hands.

"I thought you hadn't really forgiven me. And you saw"—he stretched one hand clumsily down his leg—"everything. What woman would want to look at that mess every day? It seemed plausible," he said stubbornly.

"Fair enough. I suppose it did." Her hand, so lovely and delicate, fell on his thigh. "Gideon, I have *adored* you since I was an awkward girl of seventeen. I still adore you. Yes, I blamed you along with Tarrington and Anabeth for my misery. Perhaps you even more so because…of the way I felt about you. But that is in the past. We agreed."

"Honora." Gideon settled his fingers in her hair. "I'm so sorry, for everything. For that night most of all. If I could take it all back, I would."

"You can't, and I'm not sure I would wish you to. We weren't ready to find each other yet. Not then. But now we have." Honora took the glass from his hand and placed it on the table beside him. "Don't allow Tarrington or my mother-in-law to take that away from us." She took a deep breath. "I should have told you I loved you. Because I do with all my heart."

"You love me?" Now he wished he hadn't had so much scotch.

"I thought you were brilliant enough to figure it out without being told."

Gideon's heart thumped inside his chest. "Like the Egyptians worshipped Sebek, so shall I adorn you with jewels and cherish you until the end of my days, Miss Drevenport. I'm quite madly in love with you."

A lovely smile crossed her lips. "You're foxed." Her nose wrinkled. "You need a bath and something to eat, I think. And a nap."

"Don't leave." He curled his fingers around her wrist, desperate to keep her close. It would kill him if she left.

"I've no intention of going anywhere, my lord, though Dunst was kind enough to direct me to the nearest inn. There's a terrible scandal involving us erupting just now in London. I'll dare not show my face lest I bring further embarrassment down on our heads."

She wasn't going to leave. Gideon smiled and tugged her closer, pressing a sloppy kiss to her wrist.

"I'm starving as well," she continued with a saucy tilt of her chin. "You can cut my clothes off after you've bathed and rested a bit, if you like."

"Oh, good." A half smile lit his mouth as he thought of all those creamy, generous curves beneath his fingers. He needed no other inducement to get up. His leg buckled, and she reached out to take hold of him.

"You've not done your stretches since you've been here. I can tell. How will you take me to Egypt if you can't walk or mount a camel?"

He pressed a clumsy kiss on top of her head and said in a serious tone, "Very carefully."

⟫⟫⟪⟪

HOURS LATER, EXHAUSTED and with her hair still damp because Gideon had seen fit to pull her into the tub with him, Honora listened to the even sounds of his breathing. Notching her knees further into his, she trailed her fingers lazily over his scarred hip, feeling the ridges and twisted skin. Those scars belonged to her now. She would treat them gently.

A warm hand grabbed hers, and Gideon kissed her fingers. "I'm glad to know you are not a scotch-induced hallucination."

"You're awake." She pressed a kiss to his back.

"I didn't want to interrupt the conversation you were having with yourself. Seemed impolite."

Honora snuggled closer to him. "I was only considering how beautiful you are to me, Gideon. The scars only make you more so."

A snort. But he laced his fingers with hers. "You're flattering me in order to take liberties."

"Is it working, my lord?"

Gideon took her hand and moved it lower. "What is your opinion? You're an intelligent, well-read widow."

She wrapped her fingers around the hard length of him, listening to the low growl of pleasure coming from him at her touch. She pressed a kiss to his scarred hip.

"I most definitely am. One who loves you."

EPILOGUE

G IDEON AND HONORA didn't return to London, because there wasn't any reason to. Instead, they stayed cocooned together at Longwood, far away from the gossip and speculation swirling about them.

Lady Trent visited them briefly, weeping at her part in the drama and assuring Gideon she would use all the weapons in her arsenal to put things to rights. She returned to London, armed with the news of the engagement of the Earl of Southwell to Mrs. Culpepper, an announcement that went a long way in quieting the gossip. As did the recanting of the gentlemen assumed to be Honora's lovers. Lady Trent was quite terrifying when she wished to be.

Tarrington was forced to leave for his own country estate after being hissed at, while attending the opera, for his part in disparaging the highly respected Lord Southwell and his future wife. No one missed him.

Loretta Culpepper was forcibly removed from the house she shared with Honora, when it was sold, much to the embarrass-ment of Honora's solicitor. She was sent to reside in Surrey with her daughter, who was less than overjoyed to have her mother visit permanently.

Honora's own mother and sister attempted a visit to Long-wood, finally deeming Honora acceptable now that she would be a countess. Dunst, under strict instructions from his new mistress and Lady Trent, turned them away.

Gideon and Honora spent their days taking long walks, going as far as they could until Gideon's leg pained him. They held hands. Made love in a small clearing amid a spray of wildflowers. At night, they would read together, Honora's head in Gideon's lap as he tried to teach her German.

Sometimes they argued, but rarely and usually about something ridiculous such as why a certain mushroom might be referred to as a toadstool when it was clear no toad could fit on it.

But mostly they were happy. The rakish explorer and the awkward, plump girl, who had unbelievably found each other again.

As they'd been meant to.

About the Author

Kathleen Ayers is the bestselling author of steamy Regency and Victorian romance. She's been a hopeful romantic and romance reader since buying Sweet Savage Love at a garage sale when she was fourteen while her mother was busy looking at antique animal planters. She has a weakness for tortured, witty alpha males who can't help falling for intelligent, sassy heroines.

A Texas transplant (from Pennsylvania) Kathleen spends most of her summers attempting to grow tomatoes (a wasted effort) and floating in her backyard pool with her two dogs, husband and son. When not writing she likes to visit her "happy place" (Newport, RI.), wine bars, make homemade pizza on the grill, and perfect her charcuterie board skills. Visit her at www.kathleenayers.com.

Lightning Source UK Ltd.
Milton Keynes UK
UKHW020704110422
401395UK00008B/180